**If you enjoyed Codes and Roses,
you might enjoy these Torquere Press titles:**

Bite by Sean Michael

Caged by Jourdan Lane, BA Tortuga, and Emily Vein-
glory

Fur and Fang by Sean Michael and BA Tortuga

Pack Mentality by Julia Talbot

Tomb of the God King by Julia Talbot

D1741487

Codes and Roses

Deke stopped dead, making Cady turn and raise an expectant eyebrow.

"Just how many people am I going to be parading naked in front of?" Naked and oiled. Man, it was like that one dirty book he'd read by the chick who wrote vampire novels for a living. A little Crisco, a little flexing...

"Probably only four or five, and you won't see them or hear them. No one can touch. We're on a schedule, man."

"Oh. Sorry." Shaking off the nerves, he followed Cady into a dressing room that could have belonged to a pasha or something. Water steamed in an old fashioned copper hip bath, and there were plush towels and bathing sheets and all sorts of bottles of oil.

There was also an enormous black man with a shaved head and an ear full of golden rings who smelled of the wolf even more strongly than Deke himself.

"Hey," the man rumbled, his voice like coffin lids banging in a deep, deep tomb. "I'm Jonas. I'm here to explain the process while Cady goes to town on your hairy ass."

"No waxing," Deke protested automatically, wanting that to be very clear.

Cady laughed, the sound as light and airy as Jonas' voice was dense and heavy. "No waxing. No manscaping, even, since you don't have a unibrow."

That had his cheeks flushing. "I plucked it."

"Go you. Jonas?"

"Right. Go for it, Cady."

Codes and Roses
TOP SHELF
An imprint of Torquere Press Publishers
PO Box 2545
Round Rock, TX 78680
Copyright © 2008-2009 by Julia Talbot
Cover illustration by Alessia Brio
Published with permission
ISBN: 978-1-60370-667-4, 1-60370-667-4

www.torquerepress.com

Codes and Roses
by Julia Talbot

romance for the rest of us
www.torquerepress.com

Codes and Roses

Table of Contents

Codes and Roses

An Itch to Scratch

Chapter One

Well, Deacon…"

"Deke."

The owner of the very exclusive club Deke had applied to smiled at him, making a note in a leather bound folder. The place was like that. Leather portfolios and leather chairs, the smell of expensive booze and tobacco strong, even this early in the day. "Deke, then. Your application looks perfect, and your references are impeccable. So we only have two things to talk about."

"Okay." Deke twisted his key ring around his fingers, trying not to look nervous. Normally he wouldn't set foot in a swanky place like the Bloodrose, but he had this itch that he just had to scratch, and it was getting tough to find a safe place to do it. So, there he was, sitting in front of an amazingly hot guy named Jonny, who had gone over his file with a fine toothed comb.

Jonny smiled, revealing a set of tiny, needle-sharp fangs, reminding him that he'd chosen the damned club for a reason that went beyond private membership and a free massage. "First, we need to decide exactly what you want out of your experience at Bloodrose. It says here that you would like to try to defer your membership fees by entering into an exclusivity contract with one of our current members."

Deke's cheeks heated. You didn't have to be broke to be unable to come up with the kind of fees Bloodrose charged, damn it. "Uh. Yeah. It's an option on the application. I mean, I assumed people did it all the time."

"They do. Not to worry. I just want you to understand that, barring any incompatibility, this will lock you into a year's worth of commitment."

"I do. Understand, I mean." That was the reason Deke was there, in fact. With an itch like his to scratch, he ended up at a lot of skanky bars, picking up a lot of nameless guys, and he was getting tired of it. Not to mention the fact that it was becoming dangerous.

Oh, he didn't worry any about disease or anything. That was a fortunate side effect of being a werewolf. No, what he worried about was the weird little packs of vamps and other things that were banding together out there. A man could get himself in real trouble if someone had bad intentions working, and there were more and more vamps out there who would like nothing more than to lock him away somewhere and treat him like their own little Energizer bunny.

"Well, then, we have a few options. I can try to match you with a member and you can do a few interviews. Or, if you really want to go for those membership fees, I can choose more than one patron who might meet your needs, and we can have an auction."

"An auction?" Whoa. Whoa, what did that mean? He had a sudden image in his head of some dude talking really fast and blabbering on about how he was from sturdy stock and how he could mostly control his wolf shifting, even on the fullest moon. "Wait. If someone... what? Buys me for a year, what if we don't get along?"

"All auctions have a two week guarantee." Jonny

leaned his elbows on the giant mahogany desk, looking as earnest as a vamp with a three hundred dollar haircut could look. "I also happen to be very good at placing members with partners."

"And this is the best way to defer my fees?"

"For you? Yes. You're a valuable commodity, Deke. It also helps me, I admit. You could simply come to the club on a temporary membership and meet someone, thus taking a member away. Instead, you're willing to allow me to find someone to pay for you to come here."

"Well, yeah. I mean, that's kind of the point. I need a safe place to do this, you know?" He didn't want to take someone to his apartment, didn't want to go someplace private without a security fail safe in place. Bloodrose had private rooms, good steaks, and lots of vamps to choose from. From what he'd heard.

"Well, then. I'll get the ball rolling on the patrons. That just leaves us one thing to finish up." Something in the air changed, the whole feel going from business-like to sexual. Predatory. Jonny went from all business to slinky, growly...

Deke liked it.

"Yeah? What's that?" His fingers tingled, and Deke wiped the sweaty tips on his pants legs, trying to not to get too riled up. It would make him all furry.

"Blood tests. I just want to make sure everything is nice and clean for our patrons."

"Well, it's not like I can carry the usual..."

"I know." Jonny cut him off, holding up one pale, elegant hand. "There are just as many nut jobs out there who want to hurt vampires as there are ones that wish to harm werewolves, Deke. I need to know you're not one of them."

"Fair enough." It was, too. How could he blame the man for protecting his business? "Do you, uh, do you have a lab on the premises? I don't want a regular lab getting a hold of my blood, huh?" That way led to test tubes and straightjackets and all.

"Naturally. I can have it drawn here, or we can do it the old fashioned way." Jonny moved, way too fast for him to see, coming across the desk to cup his chin in one hand. "I'm more than happy to test you myself."

"Yeah?" Now his hands weren't the only things that were sweaty. His skin prickled with heat, his breath starting to come in shallow pants. This was what he'd come here for, right? This was his damned itch. It drove him crazy, prickling at his skin like little needles that didn't have a full load of his favorite drug.

"Yes. It will help me know who to pair you with, as well. If I know your flavor. Are you willing?" There was something warm creeping into Jonny's icy eyes, something that looked a lot like need.

Deke swallowed, the sound loud and harsh. "Oh, hell yes. I'm willing."

"Excellent." Jonny took Deke's hand and pulled him from the chair before pushing him back on the solid surface of the desk itself.

A corner of heavy wood dug into his thigh, just down by his knee, but Deke ignored it. The feel of Jonny's hands electrified him, sending shivers down his spine and making his nipples harden and ache. His cock ached, too, and Deke tilted his head back, letting Jonny at his throat.

Yeah, okay, so sue him. He'd never show that kind of beta behavior with another wolf, but vamps were a whole different ball of wax. That was part of the fun, the inevitable surrender.

"Are you certain about this?" Jonny asked, and Deke rolled his eyes.

"I ain't some nervous first timer." Deke dragged

Jonny's hand down to cover his cock, which thumped with his pulse, even through his pants.

"No. No, I think you might just be a professional." Jonny's smile opened up against his throat, the feel of silky lips and the prick of tiny teeth making him buck, making him want to just fucking impale himself on them.

When Jonny finally bit him he almost came, his hips rising and falling, the feeling shooting through his whole body. His blood rushed to meet Jonny's fangs, his whole body bending to help push it up and out. Scrabbling, his hands tried to find purchase on Jonny's body, even as his feet drummed on the floor, the damned desk leaving bruises all over his leg.

It didn't last near long enough. Jonny pulled away, gently, slowly, licking his lips, and Deke sighed, hanging on to keep the world from spinning away. The pull of his blood faded, but the beat of his heart didn't slow.

"Oh, Deacon, I could simply keep you for myself. You're delicious."

"Okay." Sure. Whatever worked. He would just stay right there, jonesing on the feeding.

"So agreeable." Jonny chuckled, licking at the tiny wounds on Deke's neck. "I would very much like to fuck you now."

God. Yes, please. Deke nodded, struggling to get up so he could tear at his button and zipper, his cock beating at his pants, battering at them. Jesus, if this was what Jonny could promise him with the club, he was so in, no matter what it took.

"Shh. Let me." Sure, Jonny seemed calm, but his fingers trembled against Deke's belly. The man wasn't as unaffected as he tried to make out, and Deke knew he was right about what he'd seen in those eyes before they started all this.

"Yeah. Come on." He sucked in his belly, letting Jonny

have at him, and his pants slid down his legs, scratchy as hell. He'd only worn the damned slacks because this felt like it was a job interview or something. Not a place for jeans.

"Pretty, pretty," Jonny said, cupping his cock with one hand. "Hot. I'd forgotten how hot a werewolf can be."

It was true. He could be like a damned furnace. Some nights it made it hard to sleep, even for him. He'd had more than one vampire tell him that it was incredibly pleasant, though. They were cold-natured.

Once his pants came down, Jonny turned Deke over so he was face down on the desk, bare ass up in the air. Deke rode that feeling like the slut he knew he was, rocking his ass back, trying to spread his legs and open up wide.

Jonny laughed, the sound low and deep and sexy as hell, before pushing a finger right inside Deke's body. It scraped deliciously, and Deke moaned, his whole body into it, his entire self an aching ball of want.

"Please. Please, just fuck me."

"I'll have to put in your file how beautifully you beg," Jonny whispered against the nape of his neck, stirring the thick hairs there. Then the man slid inside him, thick cock pushing in alongside the finger Jonny still had in him, stretching him until he wanted to scream.

Sometimes he fucking loved super-hero healing. There were a lot of downsides to being fuzzy. Rough, hot sex was not one of them.

"So bloody tight. So hot." Jonny was losing his American accent with every thrust.

You had to love older vamps for shit like that. They were like onions. You never knew what you were gonna get when you started peeling back layers. There always some old world secret lurking behind their modern faces.

Sharp fangs stung the back of his neck. "Something

tells me you aren't paying attention, Deacon, despite my best efforts."

"Deke." Fuck, that bite ensured that he was paying all sorts of attention. His body sang with tension, his cock bumping the surface of Jonny's desk with every hard thrust. "Bite me again, and you'll know how focused I am."

"I only took a little the first time." Jonny pulled the finger inside him free, grabbing his hips with both hands, each movement of Jonny's hips slapping them together. "I could take a tiny bit more."

"Christ, stop pussyfooting around, will you? You could drain me almost dry and not kill me."

"Do not tempt me, Deke. I want you far more than is prudent."

"Come on!" Deke tried to reach down and fist his cock, but he couldn't get his hand in there between the desk and his belly. "Goddamn it, you asshole. I need it!"

Jonny moaned, the sound low, erotic as hell. Then those strong arms pulled him up and back, until he stood, Jonny's cock up his ass, his body arched in a tight backward arc. Jonny's hand found his cock, those fangs pushed through his skin like twin hypodermics, and the world went white hot and red.

Deke came like he hadn't since the first time a vampire had bitten him, when it was all new and he didn't know shit about itches and scratching.

It took Jonny maybe two seconds of thrusting and sucking to come, too, filling him with icy cold spunk, making goose bumps rise up on his skin.

Oh, he was so utterly fucked.

"I think we can say that you're safe, Deacon. We only need to sign the paperwork."

"Cool." Good thing Jonny was fucking strong. Deke thought his legs might be made of Jell-O.

"You're temptation itself, Deacon. Were I not too bloody busy, I would keep you for myself."

"Nah. I'm not your type."

"No? You're hot. Spicy. Enticing as all hell."

"Uh-huh." Deke laughed, letting his head loll back on Jonny's shoulder. "But I really do go by Deke. That would just piss you off."

"Hmm. You're probably right. I shall just have to make money on you."

"By all means, man. I can so get with that program."

The only problem was that he couldn't tell if this whole thing was going to take care of his itch, or make it worse.

Chapter Two

K.C. Arlington generally had no problem with impulse control.

He only had a membership at Bloodrose because that was what one did. In this day and age, procuring your own meal as a vampire was déclassé, and not a little dangerous. A carefully selected group of feeders was a better idea, and at least at Bloodrose many of those feeders were as dangerous as he was.

There was also the whole issue of work. A private detective, Kasey had to work all night sometimes, and the club provided a safe place to bring a nice meal for a day of play.

Really, though, he could take or leave most of the offerings that came up in Bloodrose's monthly catalogs. The hired help was good enough for him; he didn't need an exclusive contract with anyone.

Which was why he couldn't really understand his urge to attend Jonny's latest auction.

Maybe it was more like a compulsion.

It wasn't like the ad was all that enticing. The picture was grainy and poorly lit, looking like something from one of those little photo booths at the shopping centers that mortals loved so. Shaggy hair and a square jaw dominated the black and white, and the eyes seemed to glow like they were more canine than human, with the shine of a nocturnal animal.

The description no more suited Kasey's taste than

the photo. "Werewolf with itch to scratch seeks hungry vampire."

Who in the world came up with this shit?

Still, his fingers did the walking, and he found himself dialing Jonny's number on his cell, intent on asking a few idle questions. Merely for the sake of curiosity, of course.

"Hello?"

Kasey had dialed Jonny's private number; no personal assistant for him. "Jonny. K.C. Arlington."

"Kasey! What a pleasant surprise. You haven't been in for weeks."

"I've been on a rather labor intensive case." He liked Jonny, and thought perhaps he should make a date to play chess, rather than wasting his time on a stray wolf.

"Well, then, all the more reason to rest and relax. When are you coming in?"

"Actually, I was thinking of attending the auction." Damn it, that had slipped out entirely against his will. Where was his self-control?

"Ah." There was a wealth of satisfaction in that single word. "I thought you might see something you liked."

"Oh, I wouldn't go that far…"

"Come on, Kasey. I sent that catalog to only a very few select members. You were one of them for a reason."

"Are you trying to tell me I need to settle down?" The very idea made him restless, sending him to the great plate glass window that filled one end of his apartment. He did love to stare out, watching the night pass out in the city.

"Not if you've no desire to. However, I know that you like your donors hot, willing, and easily healed. Deacon is definitely worth your while."

Something in Jonny's tone piqued his interest, just like a really good lead in to a new case would get his juices flowing. "Have you had him?"

"Only at his initial test. This one is special, Kasey."

"Hmm." He scratched at the window with one finger, watching the little smears his touch created. "Why not keep him for yourself, then?"

"Because he's not mine to keep. Oh, I would play with him, no doubt. But keeping him would be wrong. We're not suited."

"Matchmaker, matchmaker," Kasey sang. "Make me a match."

"Sometimes it really is obvious that you were queer even before you died. Will I see you at the auction?"

The decision came to him without any thought at all, and Kasey sighed. "Yes. Yes, I will see you there, Jonny."

"Excellent. Friday at sundown. Don't be late, Kasey. The bidding on this one will be intense."

"I'm sure it will amuse me to no end to watch." As if he would bid on a full-time werewolf.

He was having a few issues with impulse control, but he wasn't stupid.

Deke stared at the red door that guarded the secrets of Bloodrose, really not sure if he wanted to go in.

What the hell was he thinking, offering up a whole year of his downtime to some vamp he didn't know? Oh, sure, there was an incompatibility clause or some such, but damn.

The very beginning fingers of sunset were streaking the sky with orange and pink when Deke finally worked up the balls to knock. The club didn't officially open until ten, apparently, when the doorman would be on duty.

"Deacon?" asked the man who opened the door, a big guy with bulging arms.

"Deke, yeah."

"Cool. Come on in, man. There's a whole team waiting to get you ready."

A whole team. Jesus. His mouth went dry, and he almost tucked his tail between his legs and ran. He couldn't, though. When the door closed behind him, shutting out what was left of the sun, Jonny came out of a back room, hand held out to shake with him.

"Deke! I'm glad you made it."

"I have a contract, huh?" That was flippant, but it was the best he could do.

"Yes, well, I've never held anyone responsible if they run off before the auction actually happens." Jonny held his hand a moment, then turned and tugged him across the main floor of the club. "Come on. We're doing this in the private rooms."

There was no more time to worry about it when Jonny dropped him off in front of a pretty little boy with purple hair, one hand sliding over the boy's ass, then patting Deke's.

"Get him ready, Cady. Have Jonas explain what will happen, huh? I have to go get the clients wined and dined. Be good, Deke."

Jonny grabbed him and gave him a quick, hard kiss before striding away, leaving him blinking like an owl in the bright daylight.

Cady motioned down the long hallway, paved with black and white tile. "He's something else, huh? I bet he hasn't told you dick, has he?"

"No." Deke shared a grin with the kid, letting Cady lead him rather than herd.

"Well, Jonas will explain it all in terms of what will get you the most money and all, but I can tell you it's my job to get you naked and oil you up."

Deke stopped dead, making Cady turn and raise an expectant eyebrow.

"Just how many people am I going to be parading naked in front of?" Naked and oiled. Man, it was like that one dirty book he'd read by the chick who wrote vampire novels for a living. A little Crisco, a little flexing...

"Probably only four or five, and you won't see them or hear them. No one can touch. We're on a schedule, man."

"Oh. Sorry." Shaking off the nerves, he followed Cady into a dressing room that could have belonged to a pasha or something. Water steamed in an old fashioned copper hip bath, and there were plush towels and bathing sheets and all sorts of bottles of oil.

There was also an enormous black man with a shaved head and an ear full of golden rings who smelled of the wolf even more strongly than Deke himself.

"Hey," the man rumbled, his voice like coffin lids banging in a deep, deep tomb. "I'm Jonas. I'm here to explain the process while Cady goes to town on your hairy ass."

"No waxing," Deke protested automatically, wanting that to be very clear.

Cady laughed, the sound as light and airy as Jonas' voice was dense and heavy. "No waxing. No manscaping, even, since you don't have a unibrow."

That had his cheeks flushing. "I plucked it."

"Go you. Jonas?"

"Right. Go for it, Cady."

The kid started pulling at his clothes, but Deke could hardly pay attention to that when Jonas started rattling off instructions. "You'll be taken to the auction chamber in a robe. The room is soundproof and the areas beyond it are dark to protect the bidders' privacy. For your protection, they can't touch you, talk to you, or ask you to do anything."

"Ow!" Deke glared at Cady, who had roughly shoved

his legs closed to get his jeans down and off. "A robe."

"Yes. Once you're in the chamber, you're to remove the robe and hand it through to Cady, who will keep it for you until the auction is over."

"Okay, then what?" He held his arms up when Cady insisted, his shirt going flying.

"Then you make sure you give a good twenty seconds to each panel of the room, which are viewing windows. Count it off in your head. After that, you're welcome to just stand there, or really ham it up."

Oink, oink. No way was he going to flex and shake his ass for a bunch of strangers. "Will it disappoint them if I just stand there?"

"Nah," Cady said, patting his ass in a friendly way. "There's no way you'll disappoint with what you're packing, stud."

Jesus. The whole thing had started to take on a real sense of unreality. His nipples were tight, though, and his cock was growing, so it was hard to deny how this was turning him on.

Jonas' nostrils flared, and the man licked his pretty lips, eyes glowing a little in the soft light. "You'll do fine. The bidding can last anywhere from five minutes to an hour. Depends on who wants you and how bad."

A wet washcloth slapped against his belly, Cady working it up across his torso. Fuck, that felt clammy.

"And after the auction?" Deke laughed sharply, Cady's touch under his arms tickling horribly.

"You'll get to meet your new mentor in a private, but monitored, setting, just to make sure everyone is getting along. Jonny will be watching your meet personally."

"Too bad," Cady murmured, running the wet cloth over Deke's privates. "Jonas and I could do a good job watching you, and enjoy it, too. Should I use any enhancements, Jonas?"

"Enhancements?" That sounded ominous.

Jonas smiled, showing a lot of teeth. "Nipple clamps, plugs, cock rings. Up to you, really, but sometimes it helps raise the price."

His cock jumped happily at the idea of a plug. "Yeah? Well, clamps and shit aren't my thing, but I could go for a plug. Might as well reflect my real tastes, huh?"

"Smart man." Jonas waved a hand, and Cady bounced, getting a new cloth and cleaning Deke's ass very thoroughly. "Something big enough to keep in, small enough to be comfortable, huh, Cady?"

"You bet. Okay, into the bath."

Time it was all said and done, Deke felt like a steamed lobster mixed with a groomed poodle. His skin shone with oil, and even his teeth had been brushed for him. Christ. All the time his cock stayed hard, too, so he couldn't even say he didn't like it.

"Now for the plug, huh?" Cady was getting breathless, the front of his faded jeans tenting out.

"Yeah." Deke gave the kid a squeeze. "You like your job, huh?"

"Well, duh. Why else would I be here? Jonas and I get to play once you're in the box."

The box. Yeah, this was sounding more and more stupid all the time. Cady pulled a case out of one of the armoires that lined the wall, showing him a black plug that would fit him perfectly. The kid was a natural.

"How much oil do you like?"

"Not too much. I like the friction." It sounded like he was saying, 'I like bananas,' or something. Casual, but for the frogginess of his voice.

"Oh, good." Cady used a tiny bit of lube on the damned thing before pushing it into Deke's body with a surprisingly deft touch. "Ta da. All ready, huh?"

A low chime sounded, a red light coming on above the

door to the dressing room. "Perfect timing, too," Jonas said. "The very first thing your new patron will ask is for you to provide a safeword. Think hard about what you want, okay?"

"Yeah. Yeah, sure." He cleared his throat, his cock suddenly trying to shrink up a bit.

"Don't be nervous," Cady said, wrapping him in the robe and reaching between its edges to stroke Deke's cock back to full hardness. "They're gonna love you."

Shit. Deke sure as hell hoped so. There wasn't any going back now. His ass muscles clenched around the plug, giving his body a little pulse of pleasure.

Looked like it was time to go play.

Chapter Three

K asey never fidgeted. He could be as still as the night, not even a breath swelling his chest to give him away if he was watching a subject on a stakeout.

So why was he crossing and uncrossing his legs impatiently and tapping his auction program on his knee? There were three offerings listed on the auction ticket tonight, but Kasey had skipped the first two, arriving just in time for Jonny to seat him in a private viewing box and tell him how to place his bid electronically.

It was fucking ridiculous to be so excited about someone he'd never met, and probably wouldn't bid on. Of course, he was already having to rationalize how it should have felt tawdry, but it didn't.

A young waiter came around with a tray, offering him a variety of beverages, but Kasey declined, tapping his fingers against the table impatiently. When the lights finally came on in the auction room, Kasey sat forward in his seat, leaning one elbow on the little table. Jonny had assured him that the glass worked like a two-way mirror, and that there was no way the man inside could see him.

The man who stepped inside simply took his breath away, and that was before the heavy white robe came off, handed through the invisible doorway that led into the brightly lit glass cube.

Broad through the shoulders, narrow through the hips,

Deacon Malvais had a body built for hunting. His chest and belly sported bands of lean muscle that rippled in the light, shining under a thin coating of oil. Shaggy, dark blond hair sat too long over the man's ears and curled on his nape, and a light mat of it covered his chest, trailing down over the flat belly to bloom around the hard cock.

Oh, what a cock. Hard, flushed a deep red, Deacon's cock stood proudly away from his body, curled up toward his chest in a gentle arc. Christ. Oh, Christ. When Deacon turned away from Kasey's window, he presented an ass you could bounce quarters off of, along with what was obviously the tip of a very fat plug.

Kasey was sold. Right then and there, and it didn't matter to him one bit what the cost turned out to be.

Turning the little keypad toward him, Kasey entered an outrageous sum, hoping against hope that the bidding would end before it truly began.

It took nearly five minutes, during which no other bids showed on the little screen, before Kasey got the confirmation, a little green light flashing on the LCD. He only noticed it because as soon as it flashed, the door to Deacon Malvais' little glass room opened, and the man was led away, leaving Kasey with a dry mouth, a hard cock, and nothing else to look at.

The door to his private cubicle opened, Jonny's low laughter filling the space. "Somehow I thought you would at least make it sporting, Kasey."

Kasey shrugged. "I want him."

"Well, he's all yours. Is there anything you'd like for us to do before you meet him? We've arranged one of the private rooms for your use for the night."

"A steak dinner."

Jonny tilted his head. "The way to his wolf's heart is through his belly, huh?"

"No. I was thinking he'd need the iron, actually."

Kasey smiled, feeling his fangs drop a lot farther than usual, but not able to care a bit.

"I'm glad you like him, Kasey. I'll give you a moment to compose yourself, and send Benny to fetch Deke when everything is ready."

"Thanks, Jonny."

"Don't mention it." Jonny started to wave him off with an airy smile, but Kasey stopped him with a tiny bit of mental pressure.

"No, Jonny. I mean it. Thank you for looking out for me."

"You've been lonely, Kasey." That was all Jonny said before slipping out the door, and really, could anyone blame him if he thought Jonny was the least likely relationship counselor in the world?

Kasey never fidgeted. Not a bit. He did this time, while he waited for Deacon Malvais. Somehow it just seemed only right.

Deke put the robe back on, letting Cady smooth it into place for him.

"Did I do good, kid? Were you and Jonas watching?"

"We were. Jonny said it wouldn't take long and not to get too busy." Cady took his arm, leaning on him and chuckling. "You did great. I like that you didn't camp it up. You're hot, as-is."

"Thanks." Someone obviously thought so, because even Deke knew very little time had passed once he went into the weirdest little glass box he ever hoped to have to stand in.

Cady led him to a solid wood door and knocked, and Deke's nostrils flared. Sweet Jesus. He smelled musk and need, and something very much like very rare red meat.

"Someone's having a steak?"

"You are," Cady said. "Rare filet. Have fun, man."

"Thanks."

Cady left him standing at the door, and it took a few agonizing minutes for it to open, leaving Deke thinking he was being stood up. Then the door opened, and Deke went from a low boil to overheated in no time.

The guy standing in front of him wore a dark green silk dressing gown over a pale, lean body. His hair screamed stereotypical vamp, dark black and long enough to flow past his shoulders, but there were no light roots, and the color wasn't dull and flat. It had all the gloss of a starling in the sunshine.

Dark brown eyes appraised him, testing him from head to toe, and he was suddenly acutely grateful for the robe, which might not cover his hard on completely, but it did keep him from feeling so much like meals on wheels or something.

"Deacon Malvais," he said, sticking out a hand, and didn't his big old paw feel fucking huge next to the other man's long, slender one?

"K.C. Arlington. Kasey. It's a pleasure to meet you, Deke. It is Deke, yes?"

"Yeah. Yeah, it is. Deacon always makes me think of churches were people speak tongues and shit."

"Right." K.C. might seem like a cool customer, but he was holding Deke's hand in a grip tight enough to leave marks. "I took the liberty of ordering you a steak. I hope that's all right. Also, I'll need to know your safeword."

"It smells great." Deke shifted from foot to foot, feeling awkward as hell. "And I'm not really the safeword type, but we'll use albino."

Okay, so it would be nice if they could go sit or something.

"Oh, shit. Come in, why don't you?" Kasey smiled,

giving him a self-deprecating laugh. "I'm a little dumbfounded, actually."

"What by?" They went inside the opulent little room, which had a tiny table for two with all the trimmings, a jetted bath on a raised dais in one corner, and a plush looking bed piled high with pillows.

Sweet.

A hell of a lot sweeter than his usual set up, which was an alley behind a club somewhere.

"By everything, I'm afraid. I generally have very good impulse control. This is not something I would ever think of, this whole auction scenario."

"Yeah, well, trust me, sometimes you just have to scratch an itch." There was something about this guy that made his mouth dry, made his skin itch. Deke felt almost like he needed to shift, like his whole body wanted to get in on the act of getting to know this man.

He really did get the whole impulse control thing, or lack thereof.

"So. Steak? I wasn't sure if you were a wine or beer man, so I ordered you both."

"Thanks." Deke smoothed the robe down the fronts of his thighs and headed for the table, feeling the plug up his as ass shift with every step. This whole thing was nuts. Crazy. Looney Tunes.

Right?

He sat with a thump, his entire body shivering with the impact.

"So, uh… What do you do, Kasey?"

"I'm a private detective. You?"

"Courier." Two jobs that went great together. Score one for Jonny, who had assured him that whoever bought his contract out would have similar interests.

"Bonded?"

Deke nodded. "Insured."

"Cool."

The steak saved him from making any more of a fool of himself, because when he lifted the cover off the plate, all he could do was dig in. The club made damned good food, which was funny, considering how many vamps were around.

Or maybe not. Someone had to feed all those donors.

"Tell me what you get out of this, Deke?" Kasey finally asked when Deke was almost finished eating.

"Huh?" He paused, fork halfway to his mouth, the steak dripping a little. It wasn't like he had forgotten Kasey was there; his persistent hard on reminded him of that like, every two seconds. He just hadn't expected navel gazing.

"What do you get out of this whole deal? I mean, I get fed as much as you can stand it, for a whole year. That's nothing to sneeze at."

"Achoo." Deke grinned at Kasey's delicately arched brow. "Look. I'm not gonna sugar coat anything. I like to get bit. I like it a lot. It makes me come. I just needed a safe way to go about it."

"Well, then." Kasey toyed with a wine glass, lips curled into a tiny smile. "Jonny tells me we have two weeks to become acquainted with one another, but I'm not sure it will take us that long to know if we're compatible."

"No?" His heart kicked up a notch in its beat, and he could tell Kasey heard it.

"No. I think we'll find out in the next five minutes, in fact." Kasey slid back from the table, moving with an animal sort of grace, dark hair moving like the man was underwater.

Dude. Was that like a vamp skill? Little Mermaid on the move.

Chuckling, Deke watched Kasey settle on the bed and pull the dressing robe open. Oh, hell yes. Lean, but muscled. Pale as milk. Sweet.

"Come feed me, Deke. I want to see how you taste."

His cock jerked, and Deke got up, dropping the robe on the way to the bed. No sense in pretending that wasn't what he was there for, because damn. He settled next to Kasey, surprised to find the man warm to the touch when he slid a hand up one thigh.

"We're not all frozen like Jonny," Kasey said, noting his tiny start. "He's kind of special."

"He is." Jonny was something else.

One of Kasey's arms wrapped around his waist, long fingers sliding along his ribs. "You're not just lukewarm, though, Deke. You're hot as fire."

"You're not helping with that. I mean, you're making me crazy." Deke wasn't sure if he should let Kasey in on that, but they were supposed to be getting to know each other, right?

"Oh, I imagine it's as much the plug and the auction that's got you up." But Kasey's fingers moved down his hip, around his belly to his cock, stroking him up and down.

"That's part of it, sure. I've had guys that left me cold, though." There had been a few vamps who had just had that lizard stare, that icy look that told Deke they'd just as soon drain him dry.

"Well, I have to admit I'm pleased to know that." Kasey smiled, showing his fangs, which were little bigger than Jonny's, a little less needle-like. Sometimes it seemed like there were a few different kinds of vamps. Or maybe they were like people, or dogs, or even wolves. They just turned out differently depending on what they were like to begin with.

"Good. That feels... Are you gonna bite me?"

"Yes." Kasey pulled Deke's face against his shoulder, settling him comfortably, before licking along his neck, finding the pulse that beat way too fast. Deke's heart felt like it was slamming against his ribs, and they hadn't even started yet.

Compatible?

Kasey was going to burn him up and leave him in ashes.

Chapter Four

Kasey let the flavor of Deke explode over his tongue. It was all salt, all heat. Animalistic and male. Christ. He wanted more, wanted to sink his fangs so deep that they'd never come free again.

Deke had an extraordinary effect on him. Period.

Instead, he waited, brushing his teeth back and forth over that sweet skin, the goose bumps feeling rough under his tongue. Goose bumps. For him. Kasey hummed, rubbing his thumb over the wet head of Deke's cock, feeling it jump and dance for him.

He might not live through this. It might just be too good.

"Thought you were going to bite me," Deke said, pushing up against his mouth.

"I am." He said it open-mouthed, closing his eyes and sinking his fangs deep into Deke's flesh, tapping the vein he so desperately wanted.

Heat. Pure fire. Spice. Kasey could swear he saw Deke, running beneath the moon, fully shifted into a huge wolf. Beautiful.

It went on and on until his ears rang with it, until Deke was growling and pushing against him, harder and harder with each beat of that strong heart. Jesus.

Deke finally moaned, bucking hard against him, and he felt it when Deke came, hot spunk falling against his leg and belly. Kasey swallowed one last gulp before pulling away, only then realizing how hard he was, how ready he was to blow, just like Deke.

"Fuck," Deke moaned, head lolling back, eyes rolled back in his head. "Again."

"No. Too soon." Tempting, but too soon.

"Not human. Not gonna kill me. MORE." So fucking insistent, so damned hot for him. Deke pulled him back in, on the other side of that throat, the unmarked side, offering.

Kasey couldn't resist if the whole world tried to stop him. A deep groan echoed in his chest, and he bit down, taking more of Deke into him, more than he'd taken of another person in many, many years.

Since he'd stopped killing for sport.

"Killing for sport, huh?" Deke murmured when he pulled away again. One of Deke's hands was clenched in his hair, holding a whole fistful of the heavy stuff.

"Once. Long ago. You've done your share." He'd seen it when he drank, Deke hunting, taking down his prey.

"Uh-huh. So. You think we're compatible?"

Kasey laughed, licking at the second set of bruises, closing the wounds. Somewhere in there he'd shot like the proverbial ton of bricks, but he'd hardly noticed. The taste of Deke had completely overwhelmed him.

"I'd say we have a good start, Deke. A very good start indeed."

It was two weeks before Deke saw Kasey again.

Hell, it wasn't like he was trying to stay away. He'd taken a delivery job that kept him out of town with a fucking locked case attached to his wrist. For a week.

Then he'd called Jonny, trying to arrange a meet at the club, and he'd found out that Kasey was on an extended stakeout.

Damn it all. Wasn't he supposed to get his itch scratched when he needed it?

"You mean I can't come in like a regular member and donate a little?" he'd asked, knowing he sounded pleading, not knowing what else to do.

"Well, you did sign a contract. Call him."

Deke cleared his throat. "I, uh, didn't get his number."

"Jesus, Deacon. What kind of fool are you?"

Bristling, Deke growled, not willing to let Jonny insult his ass. "I was a little out of it. He took a good bit."

It had been Kasey who'd left him there at the crack of dawn, asleep on the bed in the private room. Man could have woken him up to say goodbye, but nooo.

"I'll make sure he gets the message."

When he finally got the call, he was pacing back and forth in front of the picture window that was the one good thing about his fleabag apartment, staring out at the moon, which was waxing, pretty close to cycling into full.

The phone jangled his nerves even more, and Deke almost threw the handset across the room rather than answer it.

"Hello?"

"Deke."

The smooth, even sound of Kasey's voice set him back on his heels, easing him automatically.

"Well, hey. You get done with your stakeout? Is that even a good term to use with a vamp?"

"It's as good as any, and I did. I want to see you."

That had the hair going up on the back of his neck, and his cock rising like the moon outside. "Well, what if I'm busy?"

"Jonny told me about your itch. I bet you can reschedule."

"Yeah. Yeah, I bet I can. When?"

"In an hour. Sun will be long gone by then."

"Bloodrose?"

"Yes." Kasey laughed, the sound a little raw. "I don't want to be interrupted."

"Yeah, okay. I get that. See you then."

He hung up, knowing he'd lose his little bit of hard-won casualness if he didn't. Then he slipped on his best leather jacket and headed out. He'd go have a drink at the bar, wait for Kasey there. Just in case the man showed up early.

The doorman let him in, and Cady met him just inside, looking as young and sweet as ever. What the hell did he expect, though? It had been two weeks.

"Hi, Deke. Would you like a drink? Table or bar?"

"Table, I think. And yeah, a scotch and soda."

"Excellent. Have a seat over here." Cady got him seated, kissed his cheek, and headed off to get his drink. That was seriously service with a smile. Deke kind of liked the kid.

Cady was back in no time, handing over his drink, settling in across from him. "What do you need tonight, Deke? Is Mr. Arlington coming? Do you need a room?"

"If they're not all booked, then yeah. That would be great."

"Not at all. It's kind of slow." Cady leaned in. "I have to tell you, your auction was kind of awesome."

"How so?"

"You got the highest single bid ever."

Huh. Deke's cheeks heated, but it was hard to say if it was from pleasure or embarrassment. "Good to know."

"Also something he had no right to divulge. Go prepare that room, Cady."

Jonny stood there in all his pale glory, giving Deke a cool smile. Deke gestured to the seat Cady scampered to vacate.

"It's good to know how much interest he had, especially as I haven't seen hide nor hair of him."

"Yes, well, whose fault is that?" Jonny leaned his head on one hand. "Really, Deke, you failed to get his phone number."

Damn it, he knew that had probably been his responsibility, since Kasey was paying his way and all, but... "He rocked my world, man."

"Good. I hope you rocked his, too."

"He left me. Asleep."

"How rude." Jonny pursed his lips. "Which is actually something of a good sign."

"Huh?" Okay, he was officially lost.

"Well, Kasey is rather well-versed in the social niceties. If he was worried about what to say to you, and he just slipped out, then he must have been somewhat overwhelmed by you."

"Well, that's cool, I guess. Can I have a steak?"

"Certainly."

Jonny was still there, watching him lick his fork with a hot sort of predatory interest, when Kasey came in. Deke knew it the minute the man walked through the door. He could smell it.

Even if Kasey did take his sweet time making his way over.

"Jonny. Deke."

Well, hello, my name is curt and snarly. Curt Snarly... Heh. Deke grinned, letting his canines show.

"Hey. You're late."

"And it appears you were early. Thank you for entertaining him, Jonny."

"Oh, it was entirely my pleasure. Deke. Kasey." Jonny nodded and vacated the spot across the table.

Deke made to get up, but Kasey stayed him with a

raised hand. "We're supposed to be exclusive, you know. I don't care who you sleep with, but I won't have you feeding him."

"Huh?" Dumbfounded, Deke stared. "Wait. You leave me without even giving me your number, and suddenly I'm spreading myself around?"

Kasey stared at him, dark brown eyes ablaze. "Has he had you?"

"That's beside the point."

Christ, if the man was going to be a psycho, Deke needed to know. His trial period was almost up.

"No, it's not. Has he had you?"

"Yes. But not since the day I applied for club membership, okay? Just the once."

"Strangely enough, I have only had you the once. Something I intend to rectify. Shall we adjourn to the private room?"

Deke paused, torn between being damned offended and turned on. Maybe Kasey was just the type who didn't want anyone playing with his toys, no matter what they meant to him. Or maybe it meant he actually liked Deke enough to give as shit.

"Sure." Deke turned and led the way, trying not to get grumpy. He should really try to go with hot, because that would be better for both of them in the long run.

Cady fell in before them, leading Deke to the private room, smiling and opening the door for them. "If we can get you anything, gentlemen, just call. Good night."

The door closed behind them, Cady's footsteps fading, and Deke turned to look at Kasey, surprised as hell when the man grabbed him and pushed him back against the door. The kiss rocked him back on his heels, making him moan, and he grabbed Kasey's arms, holding on tight.

When Kasey finally drew back, Deke felt bruised and dazed, his knees a little weak. "Damn. Miss me?"

"You could say that." Baring his teeth, Kasey snarled, the sound almost more animal than vamp. "So hungry, Deke."

Jesus. "Didn't you eat the whole time I was gone?"

He didn't have to ask, really. He could see it now that they were up close and personal. Kasey's pale skin stretched over his cheeks too tightly, blue veins showing underneath.

"I've been damned busy," Kasey said, stepping back and crossing his arms over his chest. "Strip."

"Excuse me?" Damn. He wasn't a fucking slave.

"We have a contract. Do it." Those dark brown eyes never left his, but Deke didn't back down.

"You don't own me. We have a contract that says I feed you in return for my club fees. I'm not some little sub off the street."

"Deke..." Kasey held out one hand, but couldn't quite finish the plea.

It was there, though, unspoken, and Deke figured that was good enough. He took Kasey's hand and moved close, leaning in for one more kiss. "You do it. Get me naked, Kasey."

"Yes." Long, nimble fingers plucked at his clothes, Kasey getting him naked in seconds, loving on him with tiny little strokes. Every exposed piece of skin was touched and explored, Kasey's hands like magic, and with each touch, Deke lost a little more of his anger.

By the time his jeans hit the floor, Deke was feeling like a new man, and he sank to the floor, rubbing his cheek against the bulge in Kasey's pants.

"No. No, Deke. I need to feed. Then you can suck me all you want."

Deke stared up, reading the hunger that clouded Kasey's eyes, slurring the man's speech a little. So he tugged Kasey right down on the floor with him, falling back on his ass and spreading his thighs wide. "How about right here?" he asked, opening up a cut on his thigh, right next to the artery he knew Kasey would find so easily.

Those pupils dilated so wide they almost swallowed Kasey's irises, and the man bent and struck like a snake, fangs flashing, slipping into his skin like a hot knife through butter. The pain burst through Deke, huge and hot like demon's claws. Then the pain morphed, hardening his cock and taking his breath away.

Kasey fed and fed, making him light-headed, sending his pulse into a thready rhythm. He pushed his hands into Kasey's hair, needing more, his whole body arching up to rub against his lover's.

Was Kasey his lover? This sure felt like sex. Fuck, it felt like more than sex.

Humping against him, Kasey withdrew, then thrust in again, sucking strongly, really making Deke feel it.

His cock felt like it might explode.

"Kasey." He was gasping, tugging at that long black hair. "Kasey. Want to taste you now."

Drugged eyes stared up at him, and a drop of blood slid down the side of Kasey's jaw. "Yeah?"

"You said I could suck you all I want. I want."

A slow smile slid across Kasey's face, and then his vamp was moving, sliding up his body in a sinuous wave. Kasey undid those pants that felt so damned rough against Deke's skin, the smell good and right and completely overwhelming. Kasey straddled his chest, cock nudging at Deke's lips.

"So suck me."

The words electrified him, and Deke rolled his head up, wrapping his lips around the head of Kasey's cock. He could feel the muscles in Kasey's thighs tremble for him, could feel the way Kasey's hands bore down on his shoulders. Hot damn. Jesus, yeah.

Deke sucked until his cheeks hollowed out, sucked until he thought he might just die. He grabbed Kasey's ass, feeling tight muscle shift and pull. The heavy balls nudged at his chin, a little fuzzy, warmer than he expected. The cock in his mouth beat with his own blood, which blew his mind a little, made him want to scream, which would just be a bad idea while he was sucking.

Moaning, though, that he could do.

He moved one finger down against Kasey's crack, testing, and the man never tensed up a bit, just pushed back against his hand. So Deke went for it, sliding his finger right into Kasey's hole, adding a whole new dimension of fucking pleasure to the mix.

Christ.

Kasey cracked first, right when Deke found the sweetest spot ever with his finger, crooking it up until Kasey shouted. The man came beautifully, arching, rocking, fucking his mouth with short, sharp thrusts.

Deke let Kasey fall to one side, cock slipping out if his mouth, and reached for his own dick, stroking madly. Soon he would have to get Kasey to fuck him, but for now there was too much damned energy zinging through him, too much of his fix left over to ignore.

Another hand joined his, Kasey moaning against his shoulder, stroking him up and down, and Deke felt his balls draw up, felt it right at the base of his spine as he got ready to blow.

Jesus, Mary and Joseph.

That was too fucking good to be real, right? The man was going to ruin him for life, just by being there, just by doing what he did.

Finally Deke moaned and let it come, let his orgasm ride up in him like there was no tomorrow, spilling out over Kasey's hands. The man was a natural. Made Deke feel like a million bucks.

Kasey leaned against him, making him smile.

"Better?" Deke asked, kissing the long, pale line of Kasey's throat.

"Much. I think you're a bit too addictive. I was craving you within a day."

"Yeah?" Score. It was still all new and all a little awkward and raw, but he had a good feeling about how well he and Kasey were getting along.

Even if that possessive bone went against his urge to be the alpha wolf. They'd work that out.

Eventually.

Chapter Five

K asey hated to admit that there was anything he couldn't walk away from.

That had been his modus operandi for nearly a hundred years. If nothing was so important that you couldn't leave it behind, then you never missed it when you had to go.

A vampire always had to go, sooner or later.

Deke was proving very hard to resist, however. The man was simply fascinating, from the way he loved his coffee with enough milk and sugar to leave him jittering for an hour to the way he got a little extra fuzzy during his orgasms.

Then there was that amazing blood. Feeding from Deke was like biting a live electrical wire. It sent shock waves through Kasey's entire body, and made little lightning bolts go off in his brain. Hell, Deke made him forget who he was, where he was; everything went away but the heat and spice and the feeling of that blood pulsing through his veins.

Fucking A, the man was a distraction.

Which was bad while he was at work, even if he did just have a cheating husband and not an incubus on his hands.

Kasey sat back in his sedan and put the binoculars down. A nice side effect of vampirism was that you didn't need the expensive night vision shit. Worked for him, for sure. He scribbled the last of his findings in the pre-printed log, so he could remember it all for his client meeting the following evening, and then stuffed everything in the folder and put it in his briefcase.

He fiddled with his cell phone for a good ten minutes, opening it and closing it. Damn it, he wanted Deke to call him, not the other way around. The man had his number now, his private line.

Finally, Kasey just said fuck it and flipped the phone open one more time, dialing Deke's number.

"Hello?"

"Deke? It's Kasey."

"I know." He could almost hear Deke smile, could almost see the eye lines crinkling up. "Look, I would have called, but I'm in New Jersey. I'll be back tomorrow. Want to meet tomorrow night?"

Shit. Yeah. "I do. Badly. I want to see you. I have a client meeting just after dark."

"I can meet you at the club just after."

Deke's answering fervor was gratifying, and it made a world of difference that the man had been out of town.

Was it ridiculous that he was starting to think they needed to exchange schedules, or something equally fucking domestic like that? Jesus, he was turning into a sap. He was going to have to turn in his macho vamp card any day now.

"Make sure you get there early and have plenty of protein."

He heard Deke's breath catch. "Yeah? I bet I can do that."

"Good. You're hard to resist, Deke. I think about you far too often for my own good."

"Hey, I hear you. You make it hard to do my job, knowing I have to be away." There was a long pause, and he listened to Deke's deep, steady breath. "We need to talk about this. After. Tomorrow night."

"We do?" They did, but he wanted to make sure he and Deke wanted to discuss it for the same reasons. It could be awkward if he asked Deke to come home with him and the man laughed in his face.

Maybe more than awkward. He might rip Deke's throat right out over something like that.

"We do. I need to see you more than, like, once a month."

Oh, good. "Sounds like a plan. I'll see you tomorrow night."

"Wait. What are you doing right now?"

"Sitting in my car." His cock started to harden, just like that, which was ridiculous considering that Deke couldn't do anything about it.

"Yeah? I'm in a cheesy hotel room. Jesus, it's stuffy in here."

"So open a window."

"I can't. The scents drive me nuts. It's... it's only three days from full waxing, man."

For a moment he thought of waxing, as in watching Deke get a full Brazilian bikini wax. The man could get hairy. Then it occurred to him what Deke meant. "That could make the whole window thing a little too tempting, huh?"

"Just a little. God knows I don't want to get lost and naked in New Jersey."

"Well, no." It did make for a hilarious mental image, though. "So what are you doing to pass the time?"

"Thinking about you. Jacking off a lot." It came out so matter of fact that it took Kasey a moment to realize what Deke had said.

Then he groaned, pushing his free hand down to keep his cock from tearing a hole in his pants. "Stop that."

"What? It's the truth."

"Which helps not at all with the fact that I am sitting in my car, in plain sight of the street."

"Prissy."

There was laughter there, and heat, and Kasey liked this. This flirting. It made him smile.

"I can't help it. I'm afraid I was raised in another time." Not that he wouldn't take Deke in the middle of the Bloodrose, should the occasion arise. He surely would. That was a different story altogether, with its element of voyeurism tempered by the safety of being among peers.

"Sure, baby. Sure you were. You Victorians are the worst for your porn and shit."

"Oh, shut up. I have to go, Deke. I'll see you tomorrow."

"Night, Kasey. I'll be there."

He rang off, pushing impatiently at his cock, thinking of Deke jacking off for him and him watching. Jesus, that was a pretty image. He'd have to ask for it.

It didn't escape him that he was about to ask Deke to come home with him after their scene at the club. Fuck, that was a huge step.

It didn't escape him that Deke had called him 'baby', either.

This whole damned thing was getting out of hand.

Deke ate steak until he felt like a lion who had stuffed down an entire zebra. He really wanted to be sure he had enough protein. Cady laughed like a loon at him.

"You should just get a special protein shake from the chef, Deke. It will have everything you need in it to keep Kasey happy."

"He likes it when I eat steak. Likes the way it makes me taste. 'Sides, I need to feed." Deke gave Cady an up and down sort of look. "Need to hunt. You know?"

The kid prudently took a step back, holding his hands up. "No eating me, Deke. Jonny would disapprove."

"You think so?"

"Yeah. Let me get you one more steak…"

Deke watched Cady go, the quickness of the kid's exit almost triggering his flight response, almost making him want to run Cady down. He didn't, because Jonny would disapprove, and because he liked Cady just fine. He just really wanted to sink his teeth into something fresh, feel flesh and bone tear under his teeth.

It had been too long since he'd changed. He didn't have to do it; he just wanted to.

The hair stood up on the back of Deke's neck, and he turned to find Kasey standing behind him, still as a statue, staring at him.

Oh, hello.

"Hey, baby."

Kasey's eyes crinkled at the corners. "Hey, lover. You smell like need."

"I'm feeling it. Want to play. Want to hunt."

"Uh-huh. How was New Jersey?" That lean body moved, Kasey coming toward him, long black hair moving in the low light of the private dining room.

"Boring. Unless you count the Canadian geese."

A soft laugh escaped Kasey's lips just before they pressed to his, those strong and deceptively delicate hands closing on his upper arms. Christ, he'd needed Kasey's touch so much more than he'd thought. Just that tiny taste of it sent exquisite relief through his whole body.

"Fucking A, baby. Kiss me again."

Kasey nodded, shifting against him, and suddenly he was on his back on the floor, Kasey straddling his hips and bending to kiss him until his head spun.

That was it. That was what he craved, and it eased the

hard knot in his belly like no steak ever did.

Kasey licked at his swollen lower lip, pulling back enough to stare down at him. Those dark brown eyes all but burned for him. "How do you want me, lover?"

"Want you in me when you feed, Kasey. Now." Fuck all that prep and shit. What was the use in being a werewolf if he couldn't just take what he wanted? Deke spread, pushing his heels against the floor and humping up, letting Kasey feel all of his need.

"Yeah. Yeah, lover."

His clothes ripped under Kasey's fingers, flying off in all directions, the sound of his jeans hitting the floor reminding him that he should have changed into one of the fancy-assed robes the club provided. Then Kasey got naked, too, and his hands found that pale skin, and Deke just couldn't care if he had to go home naked.

Anything was worth being able to feel this.

Kasey's cock pushed against his balls, then pressed to his hole, the head almost hot, already damp. Deke grunted and bore down, the burn making him want to howl, making him grit his teeth and buck like crazy.

Riding out his every move, Kasey entered him slowly and surely, seating that amazing cock deep inside Deke's body, letting him feel every damned inch.

"So good."

Nodding, Kasey smiled for him, fangs fully revealed, sharp points almost shining. "Want more. Want to taste you."

"So taste me." He pulled at Kasey's hair, taking up great hanks of the stuff in his hand to force Kasey's face to his neck.

"Yes." He felt the word shape against his skin, and then there was no more talking. Only the sharp bite of fangs sinking into his skin, the amazing burn of Kasey pulling his blood to the surface, drinking it in.

There was no describing what that did to him. Deke's body went tight, his skin feeling overheated, over-sensitized, every touch leaving little burns that tingled and throbbed. The pull felt like gravity times a thousand, everything in him straining toward Kasey's mouth, including the wolf inside, who pushed, teetering right on the surface.

Kasey broke away, hips pushing forward even as the fangs pulled away. "You all right, lover?"

Deke laughed, the sound almost freakishly loud. "A little fuzzy. Sorry."

"Why sorry?" Kasey's fingers stroked his cheek, pushing his heavy stubble back and forth. "Just let it go."

Oh, God. Not one of his casual encounters had ever wanted to see what he could do, had ever wanted him to change. They'd only wanted the power in his blood.

This might shatter him.

Deke knew he couldn't let the wolf out completely; that would never work for them physically, the way they were joined. So he just let a little of his power leak through, let Kasey see and feel what he could do, how he could be the man and the wolf at the same time.

Kasey stared into his eyes, watching, stilling for a long moment. "Beautiful." Then Kasey bent and bit him again, so deep that he thought it might just tear him in two.

Howling, Deke pushed up, taking Kasey's cock and his teeth, clawed hands scrabbling at Kasey's back. He knew he was tearing the fine, pale skin there, but he didn't give a damn. He just wanted more, harder, now.

The stretch deepened, the burn making him throw back his head and howl, and Kasey slammed into him, opening him up, making him pant and grunt and bark, his whole body feeling his very own personal vamp, all over.

"Come on, Deke. So hot. So fine. Come for me, lover."

Lover. It registered that Kasey was calling him lover, and that was all she wrote. Deke blew, his cock throbbing madly, spunk coating Kasey's belly and thighs.

"Fuck! Yes." Kasey came for him, too, not quite hot, definitely wet, and all his. Head to toe.

Deke flopped back on the floor, listening to his breath rasp in his ears, his chest rising and falling like a bellows. "Christ."

The word came out as a growl, his mouth still feeling a little too toothy. Damn, he'd never lost control like that, had never wanted to.

"Mmmhmm," Kasey agreed, stroking his hair back off his forehead. "You're fucking amazing, Deke. Want to show you off. Want to lock you in a closet and never let you out."

His chuckle surprised him. "Tell me how you really feel, Kasey."

Kasey stilled, going stiff above him. "Don't mock me, Deke."

"I'm not." Shit. He reached up, pulling Kasey's head down, taking a short, sharp kiss. "No one's ever wanted me like you do."

"Good." Kasey's forehead rested against his. "Come home with me tonight. I don't want to be here at the club. I want you in my bed."

"No shit?" Damn. Okay, that freaked him out more than signing an exclusive contract for his ass for a year.

"No shit." Kasey pushed back enough to meet his eyes. "No stress, okay? It's just an offer."

"The hell it is. I know what it means for a vamp to give up his den to an outsider." It was one of the rare things vamps and wolves had in common. You guarded your safe place jealously.

"Then you know how tough it was for me to ask."

"I do." Shit. Just... shit. This was a little surreal. "We'd best get moving, huh? While it's still good and dark."

Kasey went utterly still. "You'll come?"

"I will. Right now. Well, if you can get me some clothes from somewhere." Deke let the last vestiges of his wolf go back into hiding, his body slowly morphing back into his normal human form.

"I can do that." Kasey kissed him. Hard. "I'll be right back." Slipping free of his body, Kasey padded out of the room, naked as the day he was born, which was a long while back...

Lord. He was going home with a vampire who wanted to lock him in a closet.

What the hell was he thinking?

Chapter Six

What the hell was he thinking?

Kasey let Deke into his loft, trying to ignore the little prickle at the back of his neck and the little shiver that insisted on working its way down his spine. Goddamn. The wolf was at the door, and Kasey was like Little Red Riding Hood's grandma, inviting him in.

Deke padded in behind him, nose twitching, the scenting of the air an obvious thing. "Smells like you, baby."

"Well, good. I mean, I would hate for it to smell like someone else. Or like pineapple, or something."

"You're nervous." Deke grabbed his arms, pulling him back against that solid body and kissing the back of his neck.

"I am," he admitted. "I've never brought anyone here."

"Mmm. Just me." Deke nuzzled, licking at his skin a tiny bit before moving back. "So, give me the fifty cent tour."

"Sure." Kasey grabbed the remote to his windows off the steel and glass coffee table. "This is my favorite part."

The industrial blinds opened, slowly revealing the view of the city, and Deke moaned a little, going to stare out.

"Look at that. Makes me want to run under the moon, baby."

"Did you know you were doing that, Deke? Calling me baby?"

"Huh?" Deke looked over one shoulder at him, which pushed the man's ass out in the most amazing position. Irresistible.

"Did you know you were calling me baby these days?"

"Uh-huh. I mean, it wasn't a conscious thing. Like you calling me lover."

Kasey rounded his shoulders, trying not to make it obvious that he was a little embarrassed. "Not a conscious thing."

"Nope. This is an amazing view." Deke turned back to the window, ass poking right back out like an invitation. It had to be deliberate, so Kasey went and pressed up against that muscled ass. "I thought you wanted a tour."

"It's a loft. What all is there to tour? I'll see the bed, right? Is there steak in your fridge?" Deke turned his head, soft eyelashes brushing Kasey's cheek. "Why do vamps have fridges? For their blood supply?"

"You know very well I prefer my food warm. I keep a fridge for re-sale value, naturally. And for wine, so I can seduce my prey."

"Right, since you never bring anyone here."

"Oh, shut up. I *am* trying to be suave here."

"Suave, huh?" Squirming, Deke turned to face him, hands at his waist. "I think we're past that part, baby. You can be goofy. I don't care."

Goofy was not a word most people would associate with K.C. Arlington. Still, it was nice to know Deke would allow it. He smiled, shaking his head a tiny bit, and Deke rumbled.

"I bet I can make you goofy."

Deke slid right down his front, pushing him out to lean on the window for balance, and his pants slid right down under Deke's clever fingers. That fuzzy cheek rubbed against his prick, and Kasey moaned, staring out into the night, imagining hundreds of people out there watching, seeing how Deke took care of him.

The thought made his balls draw up, even though it was far too soon to come. He needed to hold off, needed to make it last.

Deke licked at the head of his cock before sucking him in, lips sealing tight around the shaft. Goddamn. That was. Oh, fuck.

"Please, Deke. Don't tease." This was Deke, in his house, loving him. Not at the club, where they had a contract. At home. Here, in his private place.

"Mmmhmm." Deke hummed against his skin, one hand cupping his ass, the other his balls.

No. No teasing there. God, that felt… Hot. Wet. Almost as good as drinking Deke's blood. Purely sex, though, where the drinking was as much about sustaining life. Hell, Deke's blood was like speed, like crack. Addictive.

Deke squeezed his balls, letting him know his focus was wandering. The sharpness of it pushed him up on his tiptoes, the throbbing in his lower belly making him grunt.

Kasey braced himself a little harder and started thrusting, fucking Deke's mouth. He wanted to just tear Deke up, to eat the man whole. Instead, he closed his eyes against the night and humped, his cock sliding in and out of Deke's mouth.

The wet sounds were insanely erotic, and the need traveled up his spine and burst in his brain. His nipples felt as hard as his prick, his belly hard as a board. He was so ready; all it would take was…

One of Deke's fingers pushed against his hole, and that

was it. Boom. Kasey came like there was no tomorrow, his whole body rocking with it, his balls emptying with a painful suddenness.

Goddamn, it felt good.

Licking him clean, Deke leaned against his legs, holding him by the hips.

"Damn, Deke. That was…"

"Uh-huh. My head is mooshed against the window, baby."

"Oh! Shit. Sorry, lover." Kasey backed off, all but tripping over his pants, feeling ridiculous being still half-dressed. "Would you… Would you like the rest of the tour?"

"I would." Deke stood up, casually stripping off his clothes and dropping them on the floor. "Show me the bed? I want you to feed again."

"I don't want to drain you too much." He wanted to sink his fangs deep, right now.

"I had a lot of protein." Deke took his hand. "Lead the way, baby."

Kasey smiled, nodding and taking Deke off to his bed. That was what he'd wanted all this time, anyway.

They would just have to deal with the clothes on the floor thing later on.

Deke woke up in Kasey's big bed, and the first thing he did was check to make sure the damned blinds were closed. It would suck to wake up next to a cinder, and he'd passed out mid-suck-and-fuck the night before.

God, that had blown his mind.

Kasey was literally dead to the world next to him, and even though Deke knew Kasey could wake up during the day with no problem, it still sent a little shiver of superstitious apprehension down his spine. It was just the lack of breath that wigged him out.

Deke rolled out of the bed, stretching and leaping over the loft railing to land lightly on the floor below. Maybe Kasey had something in his fridge besides wine. If not, Deke might have to call for a pizza. Someone should deliver, since it was… He found a clock on Kasey's stove. It was just after noon.

The fridge yielded very little. Some water, beer and wine, and a six-pack of Coke. Deke popped one of the last open and sucked half of it down before going to search the cabinets.

"You're making enough noise to wake the dead, lover," Kasey said, patting him on the ass on the way by to the fridge. "Here. Take out menus. All of these places deliver all day."

"You rock." He picked an Italian place, because that way he could load up on carbs and protein and have leftovers. "I know the garlic thing is a myth, but somehow I feel like I ought to check with you, first."

"No worries about the garlic." Kasey gave him a glinting grin. "But thank you for asking."

"You want anything?" He knew vamps sometimes nibbled, even if he couldn't remember seeing Kasey ever do it.

"Just to watch you eat."

"Oh." His ears went hot, his chest constricting all of a sudden. Damn. "Well, uh. Do you know where I left my cell?"

"In your pants over by the windows, I imagine. You dropped them there." The little sniff at the end of that told him how Kasey felt about slobs, and that raised his hackles a little. It was almost the fullest part of the full moon, after all.

Deke bared his teeth. "Well, clear out some space in

your closet and put me in a hamper."

Kasey blinked at him, almost looking owlish with those big, dark eyes. "Seriously? You want to keep some stuff here?"

"I wouldn't be opposed." Deke padded over to get his cell phone, checking to see if he had battery before he called the pizza place. "Yeah, let me get an order for delivery. A steak calzone, a pepperoni and mushroom Sicilian, a chef's salad and a large order of pepperoni rolls. Uh… Hold on."

Deke glanced over at Kasey. "What's your address?"

Kasey rattled it off, grinning, hands on his hips. Asshole.

"Cash… Yeah. Cool, thanks." Deke hung up, shaking his head. "Don't you grin at me like that."

"I can't help it. You want to move some stuff in, but you don't even know where you are. I thought wolves were all territorial and shit."

"You have no idea." Deke knew he was still well within his base territory, just like he was at the Bloodrose. Otherwise, he never woulda slept.

"Well, you're welcome to bring some stuff. I'm out of the house a lot on cases, but I'd love to have you."

"Cool." Wow. Somehow making the leap from contracting at the club to seeing each other in real life seemed like a big deal. Deke went to open up another Coke, suddenly needing to feed his body crap, knowing that would stifle the urge to shift. His wolf wanted to come out and mark Kasey's place as his.

"You look restless. Have I made you nervous?" Kasey studied him intently, very still and serious.

"No. I'm hungry, and wanting to change. Get hairy," he added, when Kasey raised a brow.

"I won't complain, as long as you don't leave claw marks in my floors."

Right. Kasey's floors gleamed. "Do you have a housekeeper?"

"Yes. She comes in on Thursday nights. I have a standing engagement then. With an old client."

"Huh."

Feeling truly snarly now, Deke began to pace, back and forth in front of the leather and tapestry sofa and thick glass coffee table. "What kind of client? Did you get to know him like you are me?"

"Deke. Come and sit with me." Kasey stopped him mid-pace, pulling him down to the sofa. "He's an old friend. Just a friend. A vampire nearly as old as I am; think of us as old school chums."

Deke stared down at Kasey's pale, long-fingered hand, thinking how it kind of looked like an anime hand, only more square and less freakish. "Okay. I just got a little…"

"Like a dog with a new bone."

"Uh. Yeah. I don't share well."

"You don't have to." Kasey got a faraway look in his eyes. "Unless we both decide to take Jonny on at the same time…"

"Oh, Christ. That's an image."

"It is, hmm?"

Lord. That was enough to make him hard, which was inconvenient, because his food was maybe a block away. Deke could already smell it.

"We'll have to try it sometime, huh?"

"We will." He swallowed his drool, taking himself to task for letting his hormones run away with him. "There's a lot of stuff we haven't tried."

"Indeed." Those eyes sharpened, Kasey focusing on him like a hawk. "I haven't fed on you in public yet."

"You want to?" He could see that. In the right circumstances. If public meant like, the common room at Bloodrose.

"I do. Very much. I have a tiny little kink for it, in fact."

Deke filed that one away happily, pondering how hot it would be to get Kasey all worked up with some public foreplay, then take things private.

The knock came on the door just about the time he was going to move closer to Kasey on the couch, though, and Deke got up to pay the nice delivery guy, who tried to ignore that Deke was naked.

"I could go for some of that seduction wine now," Deke said, laying out his boxes and preparing to chow down. "If you'll have some with me."

"I will." Kasey went to open the wine, and Deke had his food, and it was all weirdly domestic.

So domestic that it might just freak him out a little bit. Deke would have to ponder this whole feeling, and see where it led him.

Never let it be said that a werewolf wasn't adventurous.

Chapter Seven

Kasey woke up next to a wolf.

Not an extra hairy man, or one of those super-human movie werewolves with the bulging snouts and huge muscles who took out every creature in their path. This was an honest to goodness wolf.

Gray and blond, with a lean, rangy body and thick, heavy fur, the wolf stretched across half of his bed, breathing deeply and evenly in sleep. A long, shockingly pink tongue hung out of Deke's mouth, the expression on the lupine face as happy as could be.

It was really utterly fascinating.

Kasey checked the time, discovering that it was just gone midnight. He slid lightly out of the bed and went down to open the blinds, letting the night in, and sure enough, he could see the full moon, hanging there, shining almost as bright as day.

"Good thing reflected sunlight doesn't burn, huh?" he murmured, leaning against the cool glass and thinking on the last day and a half.

Maybe he was moving too fast with Deke. After all, the man was largely an unknown. Kasey had seen him at half-wolf, so to speak, the one time he'd fed, and now he had the whole transformation, but he really knew little beyond the primal.

What did he know? He was an investigator; it was his job to assess the facts. He knew Deke was a courier. He didn't know if the job was legal or illegal. He knew the man had a fondness for steak, and that he liked his red sauce heavy on the garlic. Deke got off on being fed on, on giving blow jobs and on making Kasey crazy. Deke was a slob, who left clothes on the floor, towels in the tub, and dishes in the sink.

Beyond that, he hadn't a clue.

Did Deke have pack in the area? Family? Did he hunt? Kill?

Damn, there were a lot of variables. Sighing, Kasey rolled his head on his neck and went to call Jonny, knowing he could trust the man to talk to him, to help Kasey figure this shit out.

"Kasey! I assumed you were still busy with Deke. Is everything all right?" Jonny didn't even pretend he didn't have caller ID, which suited Kasey to the ground tonight.

"Yeah. It's all fine. He's wolfed out and sleeping."

"Ah. And you're what? Worried? Concerned?"

"I just... I need to know more about him, Jonny. More than I know, to feel the way I do."

"Bullshit. You have more than a hundred years of instinct on your hands, Kasey. You know how dull life can be when you're around as long as we are. If you like him, if he amuses you or makes you hot, then keep him for a while."

"I've told myself that. I suppose I just need my drama, hmm?"

"Yes, well, forget about drama and go take your dog for a walk. I have a club to run." Jonny hung up on him, but not before Kasey heard the laughter in the man's voice. He should take the advice, though. It was good. Well, except for the walking part. Deke was no dog, to be treated like a domesticated whelp.

Speak of the devil, Deke came up to him only seconds

later, paws slipping a little on the slick floors, and a cold nose nudged his hand. Kasey smiled, scratching behind Deke's ears.

"It's probably just as well you can't talk to me right now, lover," Kasey said, staring into those golden eyes. "You'd only give me hell, I imagine. I'm being ridiculous."

Deke snorted, as if to say, "No, you?" and settled at his feet, tail curling around the big paws.

Kasey laughed and grabbed the remote, turning on his big flat screen. "I'll try to find Lassie."

A sharp bite to his toe had him laughing again, flipping through channels.

He would just have to take it one day at a time, and let the things he did know about Deke outweigh the worry about the unknowns. What was life without a little adventure, right?

He'd worry about the rest when he had to.

Deke hated the jobs that took him away from home for more than a few days. He'd been in Atlanta for nearly a week, which was way out of his territory, and not his thing, to boot. The food was good, but a lot of the people were openly hostile, and the guy he was working with was a complete ass.

Not to mention that he fucking hated having to wear a case on a handcuff, attached to his wrist, all day and all night.

If he was completely honest, he would have to admit that he missed Kasey, too.

A lot. Like, as in pining for the man, wolf style. He hadn't even been able to call, with his temporary employer, Kyle Allen, always in his face, checking up on the briefcase. Jesus, he couldn't wait for the fucking exchange.

"Act naturally." Kyle was saying, taping wires to Deke's chest. "Don't scratch your chest. Then he'll know you're wired. We need him to verbally accept the charge of the briefcase and its contents, okay?"

"Sure," Deke murmured, pulling his mind back from his last conversation with Kasey, where they'd agreed to make it with Jonny at the club. They weren't talking theoretical. They'd set a date. Deke couldn't wait.

"Are you paying attention? We can't afford to fuck this up."

Deke met Kyle's eyes. "I've paid attention the last ten times we've gone over this. Let me do my job, and we'll be good to go."

"All right. Just pay attention to his signals, and don't get yourself dead, all right?"

"Trust me. I can handle myself."

Famous last words, Deke thought an hour later, when he was standing in front of Kyle Allen's ex-business partner, who ran drugs and who had a gun barrel mostly stuffed up Deke's left nostril.

Man, he really needed to get another job.

"Fucking asshole is wearing a fucking wire," the guy holding the gun snarled, even as the other guy tried to get the handcuff off his arm.

"All you had to do was hand over the case, man," the guy struggling with the cuff said. "Why the hell are you wearing a wire?"

"I'm not a narc," Deke said, hoping he could talk his way out instead of fighting. "My boss just wanted to hear acknowledgement of receipt of the case."

"Then he should have come himself. Goddamn it, give me the key."

"Sure." Struggling, Deke got the key out of his pocket with the hand not behind held down, and threw it as far as he could behind Mr. Pistol and Mr. Hands.

"You fucker!" Mr. Hands turned and pelted away, and Deke took that opportunity to whack the guy with the pistol in the face with the briefcase and make a run for it.

The first bullet hit him just under his right shoulder blade. The second came in just under his ribs on the same side. He made it to his truck, though, and burned out of there, the damned case still attached to his wrist banging against his leg.

He'd drop the damned thing off with Kyle, and get the hell out of Dodge. God, he fucking hated Atlanta.

He definitely needed a new job.

Chapter Eight

I'm gonna have to cancel our date with Jonny, baby." Kasey turned into his parking garage, hoping he didn't lose Deke's call, since it was the first one he'd had in maybe three days. "Why? You're back in town, yeah?"

"Well, yeah, but I'm feeling a little under the weather, man. I just got back last night."

Last night. Which meant Deke had been back in town for at least fifteen hours and hadn't called him until now. To cancel a date that was for tonight.

Color him underwhelmed.

"Under the weather how? I mean, you wolves don't get sick."

"No, but we can get hurt. Look, the job went badly, okay? I just need to have a little time to heal."

"Hurt." Shit, it had never occurred to him that Deke might get injured somehow, anymore than it occurred to him that he might. It was such a rare thing. "Tell me how to get to your place."

Kasey zoomed from entrance to exit so fast that the phone didn't even have time to blip.

"Oh, baby. I don't want to bother you, and God knows I can't feed you."

"If you think that's all I care about, you're going to be in more of a hurt when I get there. Tell me how to get to your place."

Deke told him. Kasey counted himself lucky that it

was still five hours until dawn and that he was far more stubborn than Deke gave him credit for. He pulled into the lot next to Deke's old brownstone ten minutes later, a little amazed at how close it was to his loft.

His legs burned on the way up the three flights of stairs, he was moving so fast. He all but flew, and he hadn't used that kind of energy since he'd stopped hunting and bewitching men's minds.

"Deke! Open the door!" His knuckles rapped hard enough at the solid wood door that they stung a little, but Kasey didn't care. He had a gnawing need to see Deke, to make sure the man was okay.

It seemed to take hours, but Deke finally opened the door, looking pale and pinched, his usual otherworldly energy drained right out of his eyes, his body. Everything looked dull, from Deke's shaggy blond hair to his usually bright golden eyes.

"You look like shit."

"Thanks." Deke grunted, hanging on the doorframe, and Kasey moved in to support him, kicking the door shut behind him.

"What the hell happened, Deke?" He had to scrabble for a handhold when Deke started to slide, and it made Deke hiss with pain.

"I got shot. Damned bastards must have known what I was. They had armor piercing rounds, and they stuck hard."

"Wait. You still have the slugs in you?" He got a disorienting impression of clutter and dark wood, with a few wildly colored pieces of art before he lowered Deke to the couch.

"Well, I couldn't really dig them out of my own back," Deke pointed out reasonably.

"How did you... No. I don't even want to know. Turn over." He rolled Deke over, looking at the poor, bruised back. Jesus. There were two entry wounds, and the worst thing about them was that they were trying to heal up over the bullets still beneath Deke's skin. "I guess you can't go to the hospital."

"Well, no. I mean, can you imagine what they'd say?"

The thought amused him enough to take away some of his worry and anger, and Kasey nodded. "They'd put you in a test tube. Come on, get your ass to the bathroom, lover."

"Cool. I'd hate to get blood on my couch."

Kasey looked. It was a nice couch, as couches went. Leather, like his, but without the cloth accents. They'd have to put it in the study when Deke moved in. He stilled for a moment, hands on Deke's hips, trying to decide where that had come from.

"You okay, baby? If you're squeamish, we can skip this."

"No. I'm fine." He shook off the shock and hauled Deke back to his feet, wincing at the groan that elicited. "You really need a new job. I mean, I thought couriers had to be bonded and all."

"We do. Doesn't mean our bosses have to be."

"Well, you should be more careful."

"I'll get right on that. People hire werewolves because we're tough, baby."

They got Deke to the bathroom, and Kasey pushed the man down to straddle the toilet, his abused back facing out to the room. Then he hunted through the medicine cabinet, digging out bandages and antiseptic, as well as a sterile pack with a scalpel in it.

"Were you a Boy Scout?" he asked, amazed at the sheer volume of medical supplies.

"No. You know they don't let gay boys in."

"Yeah. Good thing we have places like Bloodrose, huh?"

"Shit! Did you call Jonny?" Deke tried to look back over his shoulder, but Kasey poked him.

"I did. He understands, and says to feel better."

"Oh, good. He's a good guy, you know? I owe him for setting me up with you."

"You do." Kasey cut as gently as could into the swollen skin noticing that Deke had at least cleaned up, maybe taken a shower. "You're going to feel this some."

Once he got the skin opened back up, and blood was flowing sluggishly, Kasey got to digging for the bullets, using the scalpel and a pair of tweezers. The slug under one shoulder blade yielded easily. The one stuck against Deke's ribs resisted.

Kasey dug harder, and Deke went stiff, grunting and growling. Sighing, Kasey closed his eyes and pushed with his extra senses, knowing the bullet would be easier to dislodge if Deke just relaxed and let him do his job. There. Fucking A.

He got the last of the bullet out, making sure there was no bits of cloth or skin left in there. "Your bones seem to be okay."

"Yeah. Everything mends just fine once the metal is out, huh?" Deke stretched a little, testing. "Oh, damn, baby. That's much better."

"Good." He dumped antiseptic on the wounds. "Now, will you tell me what happened?"

"I was in Atlanta. What else do I need to say?"

"Uh, what happened?"

"I was on a transfer, I got caught wearing a wire, and I got shot getting away."

"You'll have to be more careful, lover. I like you in one piece."

"I'm thinking about a career change." Deke moved experimentally, flexing. "Damn. I should have just called you before. We could have gone to Jonny."

"No. I'm glad we didn't." The last bandage fell neatly into place, like a puzzle. "This way I get to pamper you, scold you, and offer you a job." Shit. Where in hell had that come from?

Deke stilled under his hand. "You want me to come and work for you?"

"I've been thinking about getting someone to do daytime legwork, yeah." Casual. Yeah. Look at him being casual and not pushing or anything. Live with me, work with me, feed me...

Jesus.

Kasey backed off, literally and figuratively, and Deke climbed to his feet. "What do you pay?"

"Hmm? Oh, well, I can pay about thirty a year, plus bonuses when I receive them."

"No shit... Well, that might pay my rent with just a few odd jobs on the side. I could always sell my contract to someone else next year."

Kasey spun on his heel, his hand coming out to clamp down on Deke's throat. "No. I don't think so."

"No?" Deke kind of squeaked it, but those golden eyes twinkled for him, the dullness leaving, just that quickly, the life surging back into them.

"No. You can live where you want, you can work at whatever you want, but that part is mine."

Jealousy did a lot to get rid of the need to be casual. There was no way anyone was feeding from Deke, was going to have that special, exclusive contact with this amazing wolfman. No one but him.

"Hey, I don't mind making it more permanent, man. I mean, we'll have to go to the club some or Jonny will squawk, but I could so rent this place out. I like your view."

Kasey could *hear* how Deke's heartbeat speeded up, could smell need on the newly healed skin.

"Be very sure that this is what you want, Deke," Kasey said, his hands clenching into fists. "You hardly know me."

"Shit, I've known you since the moment I set eyes on you, baby. I knew what you needed, what you wanted. Don't try to tell me I don't know now. God knows I want you."

"Tell me." His whole body vibrated with need, and Kasey held on by only the thinnest margins, knowing Deke had been hurt. "Tell me when you're healed enough for me to take you, to feed on you."

Deke reached out and pulled him close, tugging at his shirt. "Now. I need you now, baby. I'm healed enough. I promise."

Kasey took Deke at his word, picking the man up and carrying him to the bedroom, not needing directions; he could find it just fine by smell. The bed was smaller than his, but it would do, and he tossed Deke down on it, tearing at his clothes.

Already naked, Deke had a head start on him, and was already pulling at the thick cock, thumb smearing the damp drops that rose to the head all over the thin skin there.

Kasey moaned, bending to lick at Deke's cock, the flavor of musk and man exploding across his senses. Blood and come were so very much alike, only a few molecules off. It made him writhe, made his cock ache and push, and he couldn't wait any longer. Kasey sat up and spread Deke's legs, settling between them.

"You ready, lover?" he asked, hoping the answer was yes.

He got an intensely bright grin in return. "Now, baby. In me. Bite me."

"God, yes." He pushed deep into Deke's body, forgoing the rest of the prep, wanting Deke to feel him in every nerve ending.

Deke screamed for him, the sound of a hunting animal, and both arms and legs wrapped around him, holding him so close they might have shared one skin. The invitation was so clear, especially when Deke tilted his head back and offered his throat, and Kasey could never be strong enough to resist that.

He bit deep into Deke's vein, the hot blood spilling into his mouth, the power of it bowing his back in a deep arch. He shook with the taste of it, the feel of it, silky and wet. If the blood was a little more metallic than usual, he wasn't going to say a word. Not one.

Clinging to him, Deke clawed at his back, growling, humping up against him. That hard cock was trapped between their bellies now, pressing against him, leaving a damp smear on Kasey's skin.

Damn. Oh, damn, he wanted more than damp. Kasey wanted full on wet come, and he tore at Deke's throat, knowing he was doing a little damage, knowing Deke would love it.

It was like Deke had said. He'd known what Deke wanted, what Deke needed, from the moment he'd seen the man through the window at the damned auction. Kasey figured it was a good thing he had it in him to give.

Rocking, pushing and pulling, Deke got him seated deeper, gave him more blood, more sweat and need. Kasey licked at the wounds he'd made to close them, then tore open new ones, listening to Deke cry out, listening to the rough, howling voice of his wolf.

When Deke finally came it rocked Kasey right down to his core. Deke's ass went tight as a fist around him, and those beautiful eyes flew open to stare at him, Deke's hands tangling in his hair to cling hard.

"Come on, baby," Deke said. "Gimme."

So Kasey came, his whole body driving hard, his cock jerking madly even as he sucked the last few drops from Deke's closing wounds.

They settled together, Deke panting hard, those big hands opening and closing in Kasey's hair.

"Are you all right, lover?" Kasey hoped to hell he hadn't made Deke feel worse instead of better.

"I am so all right you have no idea... Did you really want me to come and work for you?"

Kasey would have held his breath if that was a practical thing for a vampire. "I wouldn't have said it if I didn't mean it. But only if you want to, Deke. I don't want to feel like I'm pressuring you."

"You're not. I'll do it. Can I start Monday? There's a few things I have to put in order before then."

"Sure. You can start Monday." Oh, God. What was he doing? Was he crazy? "Oh, and just FYI. When you move in, you can bring the paintings and the couch, but you're leaving this bed behind. It's terrible."

Deke yawned, sounding lazy and content and perfectly at ease. "You bet, baby. I like yours better."

Kasey smiled, kissing Deke on the temple. Maybe it really was just that easy.

Chapter Nine

N o, man, I can't. I'm not in the courier business anymore. Right. Okay. Yeah. We'll have that beer, okay? Bye."

Deke hung up with his old buddy Diego, feeling pretty damned good about being able to say no. Atlanta had really left a bad taste in his mouth; Kasey had really left a good one.

Speaking of, Kasey came down from the loft wearing a dark green robe and a smile, stopping on the way to his desk to take a kiss from Deke.

"Who was that?" Kasey asked, sweeping his sleep-tousled hair off to one side to sit in his high-backed office chair and tap away at his keyboard.

"Just Diego. Wanted me to run a package for him."

"Did it make you happy to tell him no?"

Deke leaned back in his chair, hands folded behind his head. "It did. You know I like him, but he always wants me to do crap that puts me in harm's way so he can stay out of it, you know?"

"I do know."

"So, what's on the plan for today, baby?" They were working well together. Oh, hell, nothing was perfect, and they fought a lot, mainly over office space and wet towels on the floor, but they were a damned good match.

"Cheating vampires. I'll take that one. Woman who thinks here Cajun sister-in-law put a hex on her. You take that one; witness interview at three. Then I thought we'd have supper at Bloodrose."

His heart kicked into high gear. They never had rescheduled their meeting with Jonny. Hell, they hadn't been to the club in the two months since Deke had moved into Kasey's loft, preferring to stay home and entertain each other.

"Yeah? Who's eating who?"

"You're having Brazilian barbeque. Jonny and I are having you. To celebrate."

"Fuck, yes." That was going to make it hard to concentrate on work, but Deke would do the best he could. "Oh, yeah, that blood test came back on the paternity thing. Not a hint of werecat in the baby."

"Excellent. We ought to get a good bonus for that one, Deke. Good work." Kasey smiled over, looking like sex on two legs. There ought to be a law about working in your pajamas.

"You could come over and thank me properly." He was pushing it, but he didn't care.

"We're on the clock," Kasey said repressively. "What would your boss think?"

"That I'm a cocksucker who loves to give his boss the full service treatment." Deke could see Kasey's cock rising, pushing the gap in that silky robe apart.

"You are. I think I'll let you wait until tonight, though. I'll need you in good form. Jonny said something about putting on a show."

"Oh, Lord." Kasey and Jonny and the whole crowd at the 'rose watching them? That was a wet dream waiting to happen. Still, what he liked best in the whole world was just Kasey. Just the two of them, together and home on a quiet night that didn't even have to involve sex or feeding.

Some days he figured the itch he had to scratch now

was purely Kasey.

There had to be a lot worse things in the world than that.

"We'd better get to work if we want to make it, then," Deke said, opening up the file on the voodoo hexing family. "I wouldn't want to miss that."

Kasey chuckled, the sound of those lean fingers flying over the keyboard loud and clear. "No, lover. You wouldn't want to miss that at all."

Kasey really didn't want to take the case. "I don't think this is about her husband cheating on her at all. She wouldn't meet your eyes, she looked the wrong way when she explained the whole situation..."

"What the hell does that mean?" Deke growled it at him, interrupting, pacing back and forth like a caged, well, wolf.

"It means she rolled her eyes like she was reading an internal teleprompter. She was lying."

"She was a werewolf, baby. We have to stick together. Pack, so to speak. I want to take the case..."

He and Deke had been working and living together now for months, and Deke had proven so adept at the work of a private investigator that he now had his license.

Too bad the man couldn't be objective when it came to other werewolves.

"Fine. You get to do the surveillance, I do the background check. Just to be less arbitrary."

"I'll show you arbitrary."

Before Kasey could even blink he had a double arm full of wolf, Deke's transition seamless, almost too fast even for his vampire eyes.

Deke was sharing the wolf with him more and more

these days, playing around at night, giving Kasey quite a challenge when it came to the chase. Four legs were ultimately faster than two, no matter what the head start was.

It was a side of Deke that Kasey had never expected, playful, all wagging tail and drool, and he found it as endearing as his friends would find it disgusting.

Jonny understood. He laughed every time Kasey called him to postpone their play date at the club.

"Don't worry about it, Arlington," Jonny would say, voice as low and smooth as truly good whiskey. "I told you from the get go that you would want to keep that one for your own. I knew you were a good match from the start."

Kasey caught Deke's furry body, turning to fling his wolf toward the couch. Deke landed hard against it, panting, tail up, then went sailing over the back, taunting him, that tail like a flag, teasing him unmercifully.

He had learned to love to play. Kasey was off in a flash, chasing Deke up the stairs to the loft, where he pounced, ending up with a naked man beneath him, not a furry animal.

"Looks like you caught me," Deke said, laughing, baring his teeth. "What are you going to do with me?"

"Hmm. I think I'll ride you into oblivion. Or maybe I'll let you suck me."

Deke's hand slid down below his belt, palm pressing against his crotch. "You know how I love that, baby. Either way works for me."

Kasey moaned, his eyes fluttering closed as he nearly forgot all about the case he didn't want to take. Deke always made him feel so good, made him forgetful when he should be paying attention. How they had managed to stay in business he didn't know.

"Suck me, I think. We can do the other after."

"You got it, baby." Low, husky laughter came to him as Deke slid down and opened his jeans, pulling Kasey's cock out slow and careful. That mouth. Oh, he could write odes to that mouth. A hundred years ago he probably would have, in a fit of Victorian drama.

Thank God for the modern age and reason.

Kasey dug his heels into the mattress, his ass clenching as he pushed up into Deke's lips. Hot, swollen, and oh so tight around him, Deke's mouth felt like paradise, and Deke began bobbing his head up and down, one hand coming up to play with Kasey's balls.

The pressure started to build there in his sac, and Kasey fought it, wanting to watch Deke suck him for hours. Those golden eyes watched him in return, Deke not bothering to close them, letting him see every bit of hunger and need, letting him see all the things Deke wanted to do with him.

Kasey put one hand on Deke's head, tangling his fingers in that shaggy blond hair, pushing Deke to move faster, harder. He needed the suction, needed the tiny scrape and sting of teeth, which made him cry out, little electrical sparks going off behind his eyes.

Deke's tongue worked him, sliding along the underside of his shaft, and the hot, wet suction made him grunt, make him want to beg, but he'd never begged for it in his life, or at least not that he could remember. So Kasey pushed harder at Deke's head, demanding instead, wordlessly asking for the man to make him scream, make him come, fucking make him explode.

His wolf just gave and gave, sucking, licking, squeezing, until Kasey finally couldn't take it anymore. Deke smiled around his cock, the look so knowing, so fucking perfect, that Kasey lost it. He shot deep into Deke's throat, his body pulsing with his release, all of the tension of the day leaking out of him.

Cock slipping from Deke's lips, Kasey flopped back on the bed, arms over his head, and contemplated why he was arguing about this latest cheating husband case. He had no reason to be jealous of the pretty lady who had come in to see them, werewolf or no.

Deke always made it very plain who he came home to, and that he waited until he came home to give it away.

"Do I get that ride now, baby?"

"Yes. Yes, you do." He rose up and pushed Deke down on the bed, moving to straddle those lean hips. He loved the feel of the light mat of hair on Deke's chest, loved the way that chest rose and fell for him with harsh inhalations. Utterly beautiful. He stroked down Deke's belly, following the trail of fuzz to the thick cock, stroking it a few times to make sure Deke was good and hard for him.

Not that Deke had ever disappointed him. Not once.

"Get me ready, lover?"

Deke nodded, eyes going a feral gold, and two fingers pushed up to Kasey's mouth, Deke demanding silently that he get them good and wet. Kasey sucked them in, making sure they were slick, and Deke nodded happily, moaning at each pull of his lips.

"That's good, baby. Real good."

He nipped one finger, not hard enough to draw blood, just enough to tease. "Now, Deke."

"Mmm. Now." Deke reached down and pushed those fingers inside him, opening him wide.

His back arched, his head falling back to let his hair brush against Deke's thighs, which drove his lover crazy, made Deke reach up with his free hand to grab a bunch of the black stuff and rub it between his fingers.

Often Kasey had wondered why he kept the mess long to begin with. Once he met Deke he knew.

Deke pushed him, opening him up fast, and Kasey took it, loving the burn, the feel of Deke pressing inside him and making him give it up.

Kasey rocked and Deke stretched him, and finally he'd had all he could take. He needed Deke's cock. Needed it hard and hotter than fire inside him. He rose up, pulling free of those amazing fingers, and grabbed Deke's prick so he could steady it.

The slow glide of that hot cock inside him might have killed him if he was human. Deke all but split him in two, and the wild grin Deke gave him when his ass met those lean hips made it all worthwhile, promised even better things to come.

As if it got much better than this.

Deke put one hand behind his head and pulled down, curling up to take a kiss. Kasey opened right up, letting Deke taste him, just like he would taste Deke soon enough. The slow drag of Deke's tongue over his echoed the deep push of that cock up his ass, and Kasey moaned, bracing himself on Deke's chest.

"Gonna feed, baby?" Deke asked, letting him sit up a little, fingers drawing patterns on his skin.

"In a moment." He wanted to ride a little, first, before it all became heat and blood and that boundless energy, and he lost the rhythm of the fucking. Rising, then falling, Kasey took Deke in and out, bouncing a little to make sure Deke felt the press of his balls, the slap of his ass.

Laughing, Deke grabbed his butt, pulling him faster, panting beneath him, reminding him that Deke hadn't come yet. Poor baby. Kasey bore down, squeezing Deke hard, making the man yelp.

Then he gave them what they both needed, bending down even more to bite through Deke's skin, his fangs sinking deep into a vein so he could pull hot, life-giving blood into his mouth. Into his body.

Deke screamed, hands clenching on his skin, cock pushing up and up into him, and Kasey rode it, losing track of everything but the burning sensation spreading through his body like his favorite drug of choice. Christ.

He barely felt it when Deke came for him, his body taking it all in, just like the blood, like the perfect hot circle of need. Kasey heard it, though, Deke growling and snarling for him, the sounds primal and deep and guttural.

One callused hand closed around his cock, and everything came back into sharp focus, his prick jumping against Deke's palm. Kasey shot for the second time in only minutes, his back arching, his balls aching a little.

Goddamn, that felt good.

"You know, we really don't have to take the case if you don't want to, baby," Deke finally said, sighing against his neck where he'd slumped down to rest.

"No, we'll take it. I know it means a lot to you."

Deke chuckled, stroking his back. "Did you ever think it would come to this?"

"What's that?"

"My little itch. The club. The auction."

"No." He'd ended up with so much more than he'd bargained for. A roommate, a business partner, and a fiercely loyal werewolf lover. "I'm glad it did."

"Me, too, baby," Deke said, stroking his back, feeling each bump along the length of his spine. "Me, too. Next time I get a terrible itch like that, I won't let it go so long before I do something about it."

Kasey bared his teeth, which made Deke chuckle. "Lover, you'd better not ever have any itch that doesn't involve me."

Deke nodded before rolling up to kiss his mouth, lips swollen and hot. "That's a promise, baby."

Well, there you go. That was all a vamp could hope

for, and the best thing he'd ever bought himself at an auction.

Life was pretty damned good.

Codes and Roses

The Werewolf Code

I got him in my sights, baby," Deke said, training his binoculars on the guy sitting in the coffee shop, smiling at some little chick with blue hair. "I tell you what, he's chatting this girl up and she's eating it with a spoon."

Sucked to be their client, if she really was worried about her hubby cheating on her. This guy was smooth, smiling and touching, the little girl just wiggling in her chair, all but panting for him.

"Yeah? Well, if they were married, he'd be cheating, but they're not," Kasey murmured in his ear, the sound of typing loud enough to tell him that his partner and favorite fuck-buddy was earning his pay.

"Wait. What?" He lowered the binoculars. "The mark and the job aren't married?"

"Nope. I've searched every database there is. No license."

"Huh. So she's lying to us." All clients lied at some point, but since this particular one claimed they were following her husband because she thought he was cheating on her...

Well. Maybe it was time to renegotiate the fee.

"I'm coming in." Deke tossed the binocs aside like they hadn't cost a couple thousand dollars and fired up the T-Bird.

"I'll be waiting, lover. We need a vacation."

The phone clicked off, and Deke tossed it aside just like the binoculars, lighting up a cigarette. He hated it when a client lied to him about why he was out there doing surveillance. It almost always meant something dangerous.

By the time he pulled into their specially fortified garage, in fact, he was in a fine rage, all but foaming. Deke stomped up the back stairs, his boots ringing against the steel grating, and hit the security lock, the palm plate cool against his overheated skin.

The smell of broiling steak hit him as soon as he walked inside his place, making his nose twitch, settling him down a good bit. Kasey knew him well. He lit another smoke, letting the pull and exhale soothe him.

"Hey, lover," Kasey said from the kitchen, overriding the quiet hum of the air conditioner and the low sounds of several fancy computers running.

"Hey, baby. Goddamn, that smells good."

"I figured you'd be hungry." Kasey wandered over to him, looking edible in loose cotton sleep pants and bare everything else. He got a kiss, Kasey's long, black hair brushing his shoulder.

"Starving. You know what rage does to me"

"My berserker." Another kiss followed, then another, but when he grabbed Kasey's ass, his lover pulled away. "I don't want to overdo your steak."

"The horror." It was a valid point, though. He hated overdone steak in the worst way. It was that whole werewolf thing. Before Deke'd been bitten, he'd liked his steaks well done. Amazing what all changed when you took on a lifetime dose of animal instinct.

"You know it. Can you get the blinds, baby? It's dark enough, now."

They had custom built, sun-proof blinds on all of their windows, a perk of old money and big city penthouses.

Thank God they got out of the city once a week or so. His wolf needed room to run, and Kasey had an estate in the upstate.

"So, she's bullshitting us," he said, cautiously flipping the blinds open as he followed Kasey to the kitchen. He didn't want to overcook his lover, either. God knew, that vamp and sun thing was a pain in the ass. You had to be real careful about nosing open curtains when a squirrel was outside.

The sun was fully down, and Kasey stared out the window a moment before answering. "Looks like it. I mean, they could have jumped a broom somewhere, but it's not legal. You have any idea how many databases I have to check…"

"I know, I know. Feed me, baby. Then I'll feed you."

Those dark brown eyes lit up, Kasey's gaze sliding down to his neck. "That's enough to make me drool, lover."

"I know." His breath started to come a little faster, his cock firming up in his black cargo pants. Deke had always had a vamp kink. Hell, that was how Kasey and him had met; he'd signed up as a donor at a club called Bloodrose. Many a vamp would pay handsomely for werewolf blood. Kasey had been the highest bidder.

It worked for both of them on every fucking level.

"Come on and have your steak. I made you those mushroom things you like, too." Those beautiful, capable hands worked, sliding his steak onto a plate, the mushrooms and onions surrounding it like fucking art.

For someone who hadn't eaten in, like, a hundred and fifty years, Kasey sure made good food.

"As long as there's nothing green." Grinning, Deke bellied up to the kitchen bar, hoisting his ass up on a stool. He'd loved broccoli once. Kale. Now even the sight of spinach made his stomach turn over.

"No, I know you only eat greens when your stomach is unsettled, you mutt."

Oh, that man was so gonna pay for that later. Asshole. Just because he wasn't born a werewolf...

"Snob."

"Plebian. Eat."

Deke ate, humming as the juice from the steak ran down his chin. Yum. He sucked it all up, even cleaned the plate, picking it up with both hands and licking. That was just what he needed.

"You going out tonight, baby?" he asked, knowing Kasey had cases of his own he was working on. Deke could do day and night surveillance as long as the moon wasn't cycling full. Kasey, though, well... He worked the night shift.

"Nope, I was going to do some legwork on our supposed Mr. and Mrs. Pedula, but if you're going to call the lying bitch in for a conference..."

Oh. Fucking A. A night alone.

"I am. Tomorrow." Sliding off his stool, Deke headed for the giant plate glass windows, stripping off his shirt as he went. Kasey liked to look out in the night when he fed, pressing Deke against the cool glass. "Come here, baby. I got something for you."

A low growl sounded behind him, Kasey coming for him, so fast and silent that he hardly had time to blink before Kasey pressed up against him, jerking at his pants, the fabric tearing way too easily.

"I guess I'll have to tell Axis that his new tactical nylon is for shit against vamps."

"Later," Kasey whispered in his ear, incredibly sharp fangs grazing his skin.

"Yeah." His whole body arched from the tiny sting, his cock waving in the air, craving a touch, a bite. "Much, much later."

"Much. Where do you want me to feed tonight, lover?" Kasey touched his throat. "Here? Or here?" Those fingers moved down his chest, sliding over his hip before landing on the crease between his thigh and his torso.

"Oh. There. Yeah, baby. There." Hell, he knew Kasey couldn't look out the window and do that, but he just didn't care. He wanted that spot. Right. There.

"Anything for you, lover." Kasey's smile reflected in the glass, wide and white and full of fangs. That shit about vamps not reflecting was utter bullshit. They were flesh and blood, just like everyone else, right?

Deke reached back and found Kasey's butt, straining his arms a little to squeeze. "Now, baby."

"Uh-huh." Turning him so his back smacked against the glass, Kasey slid down in front of him, spreading his legs wide. Those fangs scraped over his skin, making him shiver and moan, knowing what was coming. Then Kasey just struck, hard and fast, teeth sinking into his skin so the blood flowed.

There was no way to describe what that felt like. No fucking way on earth. It was pulling and tingling, so hot it felt like his skin would melt, but enough to give him goosebumps. Deke's nipples drew up, his breath caught in his chest, and his cock rubbed insistently against Kasey's cheek.

He wanted. Bad.

Kasey gave, sucking strongly, pulling at his skin, one hand coming up to cup his cock and rub at it. That hot mouth finally pulled away from his thigh, Kasey closing the tiny fang holes with a lick. Then the man sucked his prick right in, lips sealing tight around him and squeezing.

"Fuck!" His head banged against the window, his hands clenching and unclenching, his fingers finally sliding into Kasey's hair. Deke loved that too-long black stuff, loved to feel it slid against his skin. Kasey could do some inventive shit with that hair…

The sting of fangs at the head of his cock reminded him to pay attention, that he was drifting a little. Thigh muscles quivering, Deke started thrusting hard, taking Kasey's mouth just like his lover liked it. One long, elegant finger slid back behind his balls, pressing hard against the bit of skin between them and his hole before pushing right inside his body.

Deke screamed, the sound one of a hunting animal, almost a howl, his body bucking and shaking as he came for Kasey, right into that waiting mouth.

Panting, he braced himself against the window, the glass warmed now from contact with his skin. Deke unclenched one hand from Kasey's hair to stroke one sharp cheekbone.

"How do you want me, baby?"

"Stay right there." Like smoke. Kasey moved like smoke, sliding up along his body to give him a bloody kiss. "Now, turn around."

Deke turned to face the window again, knowing what Kasey wanted. His ass, neatly presented. He bent at the waist, offering, and Kasey took him in one, long stroke, pushing into him like a hot knife through butter.

They rutted. There was no other word for it. Just that. Kasey slammed into him, and Deke growled, staring out at the city below, his hands pressed against the tempered glass.

His cock barely went soft before it was hard again, ready, the tip leaving streaks on the window. Kasey's fangs nicked his neck, right at the nape, and Deke whined, a long, low sound of pleasure. He was ready to go off again, like cork popping.

"Come on, baby," he groaned. "Come on!"

"I've got you, lover." Kasey reached around to stroke his too-sensitive cock, and the whole world shorted out, all teeth and claws and Kasey's spunk inside him, that thick cock jerking and pushing, possessing him.

He came again, his poor cock spent, his balls aching. Then he hung there between the window and the lean body behind him, trying to breathe. Damned vampires didn't really need to, which made it inconvenient for him as a werewolf. Occasionally.

"You good?"

"I'm better than good." Deke sighed, leaning his head on the glass. "Ready to face up to our lying customer."

"Tomorrow, lover." Kasey pulled him up, turning him toward their bedroom. "Tonight you're mine."

Kasey closed the blinds just before dawn, wandering around the big, penthouse apartment he shared with Deke, trying to settle his mind. He didn't need to sleep, really, even if he did like to. Sometimes he was glad of it, though, because it gave him time to think when Deke was snoring away, sleeping the sleep of the alive, feet and nose twitching. Dreaming about chasing rabbits, no doubt.

He'd known the client was lying from the get-go. He could smell it on her. Deke hadn't wanted to see it, probably because she was a werewolf, and thus one of the boys, if only figuratively.

Wolf mentality.

Kasey sighed, rolling his head on his neck. He hated it when he had such a bad feeling about things, but he'd learned not to just turn clients like that down. It only led to worse things showing up at their doorstep in the long run.

He still thought they needed a vacation. Hell, even if they just went to Bloodrose for a few nights and stayed in one of the private rooms. There would be Deke's powerful blood, sucking and biting and fucking and beating. God, he could so go for that. He could go for sitting in the main room of the club with Deke riding him, too, the other club patrons looking on, some of them touching.

Stretching, Kasey went back to his computer, sitting down to check the records. He wanted to make sure he had all his ducks in a row before meeting with the sly lady wolf.

He had a feeling he'd need it.

Lauren Pedula was a beautiful woman. No doubt about it. She had smooth, cool look, enhanced by just enough make-up, her icy blonde hair pulled back to show off her angular features. When she sat down before Kasey's fancy-assed desk, she crossed her legs. The soft scratch of her silk stockings would have made any man drool, if they had any interest in the fairer sex.

Luckily, Deke didn't. Neither did Kasey. The whole shtick just left them cold.

"So, Ms. Pedula…" Kasey began, only to be cut off.

"Lauren, please." She lowered her eyelashes for exactly three seconds, coyly.

"Lauren, then. You've been bullshitting us. This man isn't your husband." Kasey tapped the picture of the guy Deke had been following around. He was big and handsome, with a smile that spoke volumes of smarm. "Now, usually we're not big on violating our client's privacy, as you know. In this case, however, we feel there may be some dangers involved in the investigation that you haven't explained."

Her face went blank, her eyes completely unreadable. "I'm not sure what you mean. I assure you, we are married."

Deke rolled his eyes. "Look, we're not gonna do the 'he said, she said' dance. You may think we're small time, but Kasey here is good at his job. He says you're lying. So what's up?"

He hated it when someone lied to him. When that someone was a werewolf, it was even worse. Gave them all a bad name. There was a code of conduct for wolves in nature, and that fucking carried over to wolves on the street, damn it.

"Very well." She stared at Kasey with venom in her eyes for a moment, before turning a pleading gaze on Deke. "You have to understand. I didn't want to lie to you, but I felt I had to. Even as immersed as you are into the anti-culture that we both represent, I wasn't certain you would believe me."

Oh, God, here they went with the sob story. Anti-culture, for Christ's sake. He hated this part, too.

"So, what's his deal?"

"My father is a scientist. A damned good one. This man was involved in one of his experiments. I believe he's out of control. I think he poses a real threat to my father's research. And… and I worry that he might have killed people."

Deke stared, his hands clenching into fists. "There's a hell of a difference between a cheater and a murderer, lady."

"Indeed," Kasey agreed. "At least five hundred a week, on retainer."

That was his baby. Always on the bottom line. Deke was a little less sanguine about it.

"What I mean," Deke growled, shooting Kasey a glare, "is that you can't expect us to unknowingly put ourselves in that kind of danger. You'd better tell us everything."

She stared a moment before seeming to make a decision. "Since you're my only hope, I suppose I have to."

"Your last…"

"My only, really. Where else am I going to find a werewolf and a vampire who own a detective agency? You're the only ones who will believe this."

"So tell." Deke growled the word out, tired of the games. He bared his teeth, and she showed hers right back.

"Fine. My father is a genetic biologist. Ever since I got bitten, he's been trying to discover what it is that makes me what I am."

Deke rolled his eyes. Really, why did people always try to make themselves more than a disease? Not that Kasey's people were any better. Vamps were always trying to make it mystical. "It's a virus."

"Yeah, but as of yet, no one has found a cure, or had even able to isolate the strain and decide where it comes from," Kasey said, tilting his head to one side. "Are you suggesting your father has?"

"Not exactly. Instead, I would say he's managed to mutate the strain in the course of trying to isolate it and create a cure." Now she leaned forward, flashing them cleavage, but it didn't seem deliberate this time. It was more incidental. She appeared genuinely imploring.

"So what did he do?"

"We're not entirely sure. This man, Jason, was one of my father's test subjects."

"Test subjects." Kasey's voice sharpened. "Was? He's no longer with your father's program, then?"

"No. He left abruptly. Just under a month ago. My father wasn't thrilled, but he let Jason go with a sizable severance. We thought that was the end of it." Her green eyes narrowed, and Deke wondered why any woman who could look that hard would need to hire someone to do her dirty work.

"But it wasn't, huh?"

"No." Lauren sighed, sitting back in her chair and crossing her arms. "Certain... mutual associates have warned us that behavioral problems, things my father had Jason flagged for, are coming to the fore. Which was why we wanted a third party, someone uninvolved, to watch him for a few days. Report his full actions."

"I see." Now it was Kasey's turn to sit back and cross his arms, mirroring her actions. Deke watched, amused and admiring, Kasey was the fucking master at this client interrogation shit. "What sort of behavior?"

"Erratic. Showing evidence of genetic changes. He's been having difficulties maintaining human form."

Deke started to boil a little, his face going hot. "You sent me off after some genetic mutant? What the hell is he?"

"A werewolf. Originally." Those green eyes went calculating for a second before they turned all blinky again. "He may be unable to control his changes now. You can see why this is important."

Deke blinked before looking to Kasey, at a lost for words. Controlling your changes as a werewolf was basic stuff, unless it was the full moon.

"I'm not sure what that means," Kasey said. "Basic control is... rudimentary."

"Not with the mutation. Did I mention he can shift into other forms; not just a wolf?"

Well, now. That was like dropping a hot turd in the punch bowl. Kasey stared at Lauren like a snake stares down a bird or a rat, never blinking.

"In that case, we'll require an extra thousand dollars a week in hazard pay, and I would like access to your father's files."

"Out of the question..."

In the end, though, Kasey won, and they had a date to meet with Lauren's father two nights later.

"Looks like you're back on daytime surveillance, lover," Kasey said, showing Lauren the door none too gently.

"Yeah." Sighing, he ran a hand through his hair. Then Deke grinned. So much for the power of a cool, beautiful blonde. He'd put his money on a dark horse like Kasey any day.

Kasey paced, waiting for Deke to get home. He'd gotten email from hell, with all sorts of data, Lauren's father being far more accommodating than his darling daughter, at least on the surface. When he dug deeper, though, it was a nightmare.

There was some serious shit there, and Deke wasn't answering his Goddamned cell phone.

The sound of big paws hitting the glass doors to the balcony made him jump, and he went to the little screen he used for the security cameras. Deke. Fully wolfed out. Huh.

He stayed in the little windowless control room and worked the blinds by remote, knowing Deke would close them so he could avoid the sun. What the hell Deke was doing all fuzzy when it was just after five and full on rush hour out there…

Seconds ticked by and Deke didn't call out, didn't close the blinds. Kasey finally flipped the remote switch again, watching the blinding light disappear from the security screen, making out the shadow of his wolf on the floor, just inside the doors.

Damn it.

"Deke? Lover? Come on, honey. What is it?" Kasey checked the room quickly for errant sunbeams before easing out, making sure Deke was, well, Deke. Yep. Blond and gray, big old wolf, not the full moon giant that Deke could become.

Deke lifted his head, golden eyes dull, a trickle of blood running from his muzzle.

"Shit! Deke." Kasey moved fast, kneeling at Deke's side, his fingers searching through that thick fur, looking for any signs of injury. When he reached Deke's flank, he came away with something sharp and metallic.

A dart.

"Someone drugged you? Jesus, Deke. What the hell were you doing? Waving a flag that said private detective?"

Deke growled at him, almost silently, lips curling back on a snarl. If his lover couldn't change back to human to tell him to fuck off it, meant Deke's body was still fighting some kind of poison, and Kasey needed to help.

"Stay here, lover. I'll get a blanket." Then he'd analyze the damned drug, see what he could do to counteract it. Luckily, he didn't need a chemistry set to do that shit. Just his vampy spider-sense.

Wrapping Deke in the ancient quilt they kept on the couch, Kasey took the dart to the safe room, knowing Deke wasn't in any real danger. There'd been no panic in those yellow eyes, no smell of decay. Just the sense of slow, and of needing to heal.

Kasey put on gloves and broke the dart open, studying the remaining fluid. The tip of the dart was thick and heavy, extra long, and looked like an intramuscular shot could be administered through it.

The stuff smelled like a date rape drug.

When he finally bit the bullet and dropped a tiny bit of the stuff on his tongue, Kasey rolled his eyes. Pharmaceutical grade downer. Probably lorazepam. In a big enough dose to bring down an elephant.

Or a werewolf.

Deke would sleep it off in an hour, but that high of a dose would have disabled him enough that getting home as a human would have been impossible.

Shit.

Maybe they should have asked for more than an extra thousand a week.

Deke woke slowly, his brain foggy, his body lax and heavy.

Man, whatever the number of that truck was…

"Hey, lover. How are you feeling?"

He blinked, opened his mouth to answer, and found only a growl. Oh. Wolfy. Huh. He thought hard about his human body, imagined his wolf form slipping away, and for an awful moment, nothing happened. Before he could panic, though, his snout shortened, his tail pulled in, and his arms and legs stretched out. Look at that. Opposable thumbs.

"Wha' happened?" he asked, his tongue feeling like lead.

"You tell me, man." Kasey squatted down in front of him, pulling him to a sitting position. The quilt slid away from him, goosebumps rising on his skin. Thank God he got home before he got naked.

"Hell if I know. One minute I was on foot, following the mark to his car to get his plate number and shit. The next, boom, I was going down and I knew I had to change. I don't remember getting home."

Kasey's dark eyes held his, serious as a heart attack. "Did you lead them here, lover?"

"Shit, I don't know. Did they come knocking?" He couldn't hear his own thoughts through the pounding in his head. "I need to take a shower."

"Come on." Strong hands pulled him to his feet, Kasey's easy heft always amazing him, especially now, when Deke felt like a neutron star or something.

Deke went, his limbs heavy, boneless. They stopped in the bedroom, not the bathroom, Kasey easing him down on the bed.

"Baby, I need the shower, not another nap. I need to figure out…"

"Shh." Kasey pressed one finger to his lips. "I know what you need, lover. I've got it right here." Head tilting to one side, Kasey offered up his neck, one finger slicing open the skin so that amazing vampire blood ran down Kasey's pale skin.

Oh, God. He hardly ever got to taste, hardly ever got to be on the receiving end. Deke closed his eyes, his mouth finding the cut, lips closing down so he could suck.

Kasey's blood was like fucking speed. It spread through his whole body with a hot tingle, making his skin feel tight, making his body arch and twist. His heart speeded up, his fingers tangled in Kasey's hair, and he drank as much as he could before his lover healed up on him. Hell, he fucking gloried in it.

Panting, Deke pulled back to look into those dark eyes. "I can tell you exactly what happened now, baby."

Smiling, fangs showing just a bit, Kasey pushed him down on the bed again, straddling him.

It occurred to Deke just then that his cock was rock hard and ready, his hips already rocking up to meet Kasey's ass. "Ride me, then. Come on, baby. Ride me."

"Yes." Eyes almost glowing, Kasey rose up and grabbed his cock, pushing back against it. So tight. Tight and good, and he loved that Kasey didn't need to take time to get ready, could take him in like nothing going.

Deke thrust up, grunting, pushing, his cock squeezed so tight that he cried out.

Kasey started riding him, up and down, rocking his world and making his eyes roll back in his head. Every bit of lassitude was gone, his body alive, the drugs working their way out completely.

He grabbed Kasey's hips, moving them faster, harder, until their bodies slapped together. Kasey moaned, belly tight, thighs trembling, hands braced on Deke's chest. When Kasey looked down at him, fangs sinking into that pretty lower lip, Deke had to reach up and pull Kasey down, taking a kiss.

Goddamn, he loved it when Kasey was crazy for him, had been worried about him. It was wild, hot, and when Kasey bit into Deke's lower lip, taking the tiny bit of blood that welled up, that was it. Deke came hard, cock jerking, giving Kasey his blood and his spunk.

"Deke…" Sitting up on top of him, Kasey took his hand, putting it on that hard cock, begging him to work it, to make Kasey come, too.

"I got you, baby." Pulling, sliding his fingers and thumb hard around the head, Deke started jacking Kasey's cock, needing to see and smell.

"Oh. Oh, lover." Kasey shot for him, wet and slick, come sliding over his hand and belly.

"Mmm. Love it when you feed me, baby," Deke murmured, stroking Kasey's back.

"You love all the parts." Licking his split lip, Kasey growled a little. "Don't scare me like that again, got it?"

Deke just nodded. Hell, he didn't want to scare himself like that. "I was following him. He was on his way to a car, and I thought I'd get you some information. The weirdest shit happened, though, baby. He just… up and disappeared. Like some weird Terminator Three dealie."

"You mean he morphed? Wolf-like or otherwise?"

"I mean he went all fluid and sort of walked through a

wall. Not long after that, I got shot."

Kasey stared down at him, expression gone all calculating. "We need to move up the meeting with the old man."

Sighing, Deke nodded, but his hands ignored the better urgings of his brain and went to pull Kasey down for another kiss. "This could get dangerous, baby."

"We just have to make a new plan."

They shared a grin, both of them thinking, then saying the same thing together. "And charge more."

The meeting had gone... badly.

"What the hell did you do to him that he can change into mist or whatever?" Deke had asked right off the bat, and the old guy had gotten his hackles up.

"He cannot change to mist. That's an illusion. He can simply make his body take on a form we can't see."

Lauren had made a show of trying to intervene, but Deke wasn't one to back down, and Kasey had finally called a halt, knowing it would only get nasty if he let Deke go.

"We can't work under these conditions. We're quitting the case."

"What? You can't!" Standing, Lauren had thrown up her hands, starting to pace. "He has to be watched."

"He assaulted me," Deke snarled. "He knows he's being watched."

"Not to mention the fact that he can walk through walls," Kasey agreed, smiling a little at his growly lover.

"I gave you my files." Lauren's father seemed to think that made everything better, but even to Kasey most of it was gibberish. "He can't walk through walls. He only made you think he had."

"Give it to us in layman's terms, then."

Things had gone downhill even worse, then.

The old man had explained about genetic mutation and introducing super-concentrated sets of gene therapy into patients and testing to see what affects they had.

"How many patients?" Deke had finally asked, cutting the old fellow off when he started to get too proud of himself.

"I beg your pardon?"

"How many people have you fucked royally? Bad enough to be a freak of nature, but to be a freak among the freaks? Shit." Deke spit on the floor.

Kasey wrinkled his nose.

"I did it in the name of science! I had to find a way to heal my Lauren!"

"Oh, yeah. So she's still a werewolf and now there's this melty-changing into nothing-freak out there. Good job, Doc."

"Out. Get out of my home. You're fired." The old man stood dramatically, finger pointing toward the door.

"You must have missed it when we quit, then," Deke said, laughing his booming laugh and standing, too.

Kasey had followed, admiring the fit of Deke's jeans, shaking his head at the stupidity of people when faced with things they didn't understand.

"Please. Wait." Lauren had rushed up to stop them, grabbing Deke's arm. "I'm sorry. We need your help."

"No, you need to get daddy to accept that you're a werewolf, honey. And a bitch, at that." Deke shook her off, turning to wink at Kasey before walking off.

Now they sat in their own front room, Deke lounging on the couch, shirt off and jeans open, looking like sex on two legs. It made Kasey hard, made him want to forget all about the cool blonde and her genetic tampering daddy.

Too bad he couldn't, at least right away.

"You think he'll come after us?"

The new kind of shifter must know who they were, now. He'd had Deke at his mercy, had no doubt followed him, and it would be stupid for the guy to go about his business without keeping an eye on Lauren and the old man. Jason had to know someone wanted him back in the fold, no doubt to either reverse his ability or lock him up...

Why he hadn't taken advantage of Deke being all drugged, Kasey didn't know. There had to be a reason, but it made Kasey nervous as hell.

"We'll be on guard if he does." Looking supremely unconcerned, Deke crooked a finger at him, gesturing him over.

"What?"

"C'mere, baby. Want to do bad things to you."

Kasey hid his shiver. "I was thinking we could go to the Rose. Stay there for a few days, just until this blows over."

"Yeah?" Deke perked right up at that, and Kasey could smell his interest.

"Uh-huh. I think we ought to just go. Play a little. We have the deposit from the last case. We can enjoy ourselves for a few days."

Deke got up and sauntered over, cock starting to poke out of his open jeans. "I think that sounds like an amazing fucking idea. It would take more than a mutant werewolf to get through the security there."

"You know it." Reaching out, Kasey pushed his hand into Deke's pants. "I could feast on you for hours, lover."

"And I could fuck you into the floor. Let's do it."

"I'll call Jonny. Let him know we're coming." Jonny was the keeper of the keys at the Bloodrose, and he was fucking amazing at setting things up just like Deke and Kasey liked them. Hell, Jonny was the reason they'd gotten together in the first place.

"Cool. I'll go throw some shit in a bag."

Kasey picked up the phone, dialing Jonny's number, wanting to make sure they could get in before dawn. He was listening to the damned thing ring when the tinted, reinforced glass of their front window burst inward, shattering into tiny pieces.

Rolling out of his chair, Kasey slid across the floor toward his weapons, reaching for anything that would help him fight whatever it was coming through his wall.

Before he could reach even so much as a pocketknife, the thing was on him. It landed hard on, him, a messy, furry thing that wasn't a wolf or a man. It sure had bad breath, fetid and damp, its tongue dragging against his cheek.

A roar sounded from the other room, and Kasey's very own berserker wolf popped right up in front of them, tricked out in his full moon form, big hands dragging the thing away from him.

"Get your own fucking vamp," Deke snarled, flinging the monster away.

Landing in a crouch, the thing turned and came at Deke, claws stretched out, teeth bared. Goddamn.

Deke grunted, keeping the snapping teeth from his throat by mere inches. Kasey had no idea what would happen to Deke if that thing bit him, and he didn't want to find out. So he leaped, clawing at the strangely squishy back with his nails.

"Give me the files.'

Hell, that was what he thought the thing said, anyway. Who the fuck knew? He could hear Jonny on his phone, shouting, his voice tiny and tinny.

"Fuck that shit. Go harass the old man." Deke shoved,

and the thing staggered back, long teeth bared and dripping with saliva.

Then it just... disappeared.

Kasey turned in a fast circle, scenting the air, but it was Deke who figured it out first. Behind you, baby!"

Whirling again, Kasey caught the slimy thing that landed against him, hands slipping and sliding on its skin. Goddamn, that was foul. The thing's breath nearly made him gag, but Kasey managed to hold on, hollering for Deke.

"Get the damned riot cuffs!"

"And put them on what?" Deke's hands closed on thin air, and Kasey staggered right into Deke's arms as whatever he was holding slipped away.

"Shit!" The thing seemed to vaporize under his hands. How in the name of fuck were they supposed to fight that?

"Kasey!" Spinning, Deke shoved him away, running toward their office.

Papers flew everywhere, like there was a mini tornado in the room, but they couldn't see anyone. Deke went right for the guy, though, nose working overtime. Kasey hated to admit it, but for a moment he was completely lost in watching his man move, that huge upright wolf body flowing smoothly, muscles shifting and pulling.

"Some help, baby?"

Snapping out of his stupor, Kasey moved, sliding in low and fast, taking the thing's legs out from under it. When the big body hit the floor, it became visible again.

This time it was just a man, naked and sweaty and wild-eyed.

"Please. Please. I need the professor's files," Jason said. That was the guy's name. Jason. "I can't... I keep changing. I can't control it anymore. Please. Help me."

Well, shit. That couldn't be good.

Kasey sat back on his heels and glanced at Deke, who nodded, his grin razor sharp and full of teeth. "Call the lady, Kasey. We got us a situation."

No shit. He watched Jason's hands go all hairy and clawed, the rest of the body staying human. That was a situation and a half.

They set up the meet with the professor and Lauren, giving Jason a robe to wear. While Kasey called Jonny back to explain all the noises and shit, Deke sat across from Jason, staring at him intently.

"What?" The guy finally asked. "Do I have something on my face?"

Deke snorted. "Yeah. A snout. I tell you what, man, you're the weirdest wolf I've ever seen."

The guy's face twisted all up. "That's hardly my fault, man. If the old asshole would experiment on his little girl instead of us idiots…"

Raising one brow, Deke stared harder. "You telling me you signed up for gene therapy and never thought it might be bad?"

"Not like this. At first, well…"

"Yeah. At first you figured you were gonna have infinite cosmic power or something, huh?"

"Asshole."

Deke growled, his fists clenching. "You're the one who broke through my fucking window, man." He'd just as soon rip the guy's head off and shit down his neck as look at him, but he knew they had to keep him on ice until the professor showed up. This guy couldn't be allowed to run free.

"I need those files."

"So why not just go back to the professor and tell him you're having issues?"

"I left, didn't I? I could hardly go back." Jason's eyes slid away, not meeting his.

"Why not? It was his fault. What, did you steal something when you left?"

"Only my own body. I was contracted for another two years. Look," Jason said, finally looking at him again. "I don't know what's happening to me. When I first left I had control. Now it's completely random, and it's getting kinda gross."

"Kinda? Man, you have poopie-eater breath."

"Ah, dog talk." Kasey came over, rubbing a hand up and down his back. "Such a lovely thing."

"Yeah, yeah. Get a hold of our friend?" He didn't want to mention the club or Jonny, just in case. That was their place, and Deke didn't want it spoiled. Not to mention the fact that Jonny would kick their asses for bringing this shit to his house.

"I did. Told him I'd call back. We've got to get somewhere before daylight, lover. That broken window..."

"Yeah. I figure the Doc will have show soon." They had a few hours, but he could see Kasey's problem. Even if they put Kasey in the windowless secure room, it wasn't gonna be safe in their place. They'd call the guy who put the window in to come during the daylight hours and fix the damned thing. The shutters wouldn't close without the glass.

"I don't mean to interrupt..."

"So don't." He and Kasey said it together, the words hard, the looks they gave Jason harder. Hell, he could see the guy's problem, but it wasn't theirs to deal with. They were just the hired thugs.

The knock at the door saved that skanky ass from Deke getting all riled up. Kasey went to let Lauren and the Doc in, both of them looking worried as all hell.

"Jason! Oh, thank goodness." Lauren went to put a hand on the guy's arm, but stopped a few feet away, scenting the air. "My God. What's wrong with you?"

"You tell me, babe." Rolling his shoulders, Jason stared at the professor. "Something's broken in me, Doc. Something bad."

"Then come back to the research center." The old man moved close, staring at Jason's skin, poking here and there. The doc was creepy in the extreme, completely unnerving in his scientific obtuseness.

"You gonna make me give back the severance money?"

Lauren snorted. "I imagine you've spent it all."

Nodding, Jason stood, holding out his arms so the Doc could poke and prod him some more. "I have. I won't deny it. I needed it to live, after what you people did to me."

"Well, you'd best go back with the doc, then." Deke crossed his arms over his chest, ready to be done with all of this bullshit. "Then the doc can pay us, and we'll be out of your hair."

"Sure. Sure." Jason cocked an eyebrow and smiled, a cold, slimy smile that sent a nasty chill down Deke's back. "The only problem with that is the people I've bitten. Do you think they'll start mutating too?"

Everyone in the fucking room just stared at the fuckwad in disbelief, but it was Kasey who went over and popped Jason in the jaw, sending the asshole spiraling to the floor, unconscious.

Kasey leveled a finger at the Doctor and his pretty daughter. "You made this mess. Now you're going to clean it up."

"You'll help us, right?"

Sometimes that lizard stare made Deke think that

vampires had come from the time of dinosaurs. It was enough to send shivers down Lauren's spine, Deke could tell.

"That," Kasey said, "depends on how much you pay us."

Oh, yeah. Fucking A.

Kasey took all of his portable computer equipment and set up at the Doc's compound for the day.

According to Jason, when he woke up enough to talk, he'd bitten three people. Two men and a woman. That was going to be a bitch, but he and Deke weren't fucking detectives for nothing. Hopefully, those three assholes hadn't bitten three more assholes and so on down the line.

With what the old fart was paying them, they could buy a thousand new windows. That alone made it worth doing the job.

"You got a line on the blue-haired chick, lover?"

Deke's voice came back over their fancy new radio system, voice a little tinny over the satellite link. "I got her. Hell, she might not even need the drug. She's completely disoriented. Asshole bit them and just never told them shit."

They had Jason's supply of tranquilizers, and the dart gun he'd used on Deke. Kasey had to admire the man's resourcefulness, even if he thought Jason should just be destroyed like a rabid dog.

The guy had taken the professor's money and run with the idea of creating a pack of super-powered werewolves, after all. Like they were the X-Men or something. Assholes like that didn't deserve to live. Even Kasey knew that violated the werewolf code, or some shit. Why Jason had only drugged Deke and not tried to turn him into whatever was a mystery, but Kasey wasn't gonna complain.

"She's number two. Only one more to go after her, and we saved the hardest for last. He's big, lover."

"One at a time, baby." Deke was on the move, the little tracking device beeping merrily away. Kasey could see that fine body in his mind's eye, all smooth muscle and prowly wolf.

"I know. She's moving."

"I said I got her."

Kasey shut up. Deke hated it when he tried to be a backseat driver on a capture.

The little dot moved faster, and he could hear Deke breathing harder. There was the sound of a short tussle, and cut off cry, and then silence.

"Bagged and tagged, baby. Point me toward number three, and we're all good."

"Secure her with the first one, and I'll give you the coordinates."

Jason had picked three very different people to infect, just to see what the effects would be. Hell, the Doc should be proud; the guy was using scientific method. Asshat.

"She's in the van." They had a reinforced vehicle that Deke hadn't been able to break out of when they tested it, and luckily, none of the newly infected bunch had taken their first moon yet, so they weren't at full strength. If Deke was right, they were all a little loopy, too, the virus mutated so badly that they were staggering around like idiots.

"Okay. Number three has an apartment at Fifteenth and Washington."

With any luck, the guy would be home, and that would be that. He was the first one Jason had bitten, a big dock worker with a terrible attitude problem.

The radio silence while Deke drove was just starting

to bother him when the connection crackled to life again. "Which building?"

"Southwest corner, number five-oh-two."

"Fabulous. A fucking walk-up."

He laughed, knowing just how well Deke loved stairs. "Think what it will do for your ass, lover. Buns of steel."

"Oh, fuck you. You can do that whole vampy levitating thing." Deke was panting by the time his little satellite blip hit the fifth floor, but not bad enough to worry over.

Kasey heard Deke knock at the door, but nothing else, only Deke's breathing.

"I'm going in, baby."

"Be careful."

"It's my middle name."

"Bullshit."

The bang as the door flew open sounded like a pistol shot, and he could hear Deke move in fast. Then his lover started to gag. "Oh, baby. Oh, God. We don't have to worry about this one. Get with the Prof and get a clean-up crew."

Christ. "Dead?"

"Yeah. It's messy. He'd better get to work on un-mutating the rest. This guy went feral. He's chewed himself to pieces. Literally, baby."

Oh, man. Kasey had only seen something like that once, when some African elemental had been in town. "Don't even touch anything. Get the fuck out of there, and don't let the other two bite you. I'll get on the clean up."

"Got it. On my way in."

They both clicked off, and Kasey punched the line to the Doc's office. "Hey, Doc. Your third outstanding collection was defunct. You need a hazmat team out there."

"A hazmat... Oh, I see. It's bad, is it?"

Kasey rolled his eyes. Duh. "Yes. You'll need to talk to Deke when he gets back. Look at the ones you have in containment."

"Very well."

"Bye, Doc." God Almighty. The man was just... well, less human than either him or Deke, for sure.

He grabbed his phone, flipping it open and heading to the bathroom, dialing a familiar number.

"Jonny? Hey, man. K.C. Arlington. Deke and I want to come and stay for a bit while we do some remodeling."

"Kasey. I was starting to worry about you." Jonny sounded like he was smiling. That would probably scare most people. Jonny smiled like a shark.

"Yeah, well, we had some issues. We need some R and R. Can we get something private?"

"Of course. You two are some of my best customers." The clacking of keys sounded. "I can have something ready at dusk."

"Solid. I'll see you then."

"Anything else?" Jonny could always read him, even if he wasn't standing in front of the man.

"Yeah. Test your donors. Carefully. There's a mutated strain of the wolf out there. Breaks the code. I have no idea what kind of issues it could cause with vamp DNA."

"First I've heard of it, Kase."

"I know." Kasey blew out a sigh. Jonny was usually the first to hear any scuttlebutt on the street. "Let's just say I know the source."

"Not Deke."

"No. No, no. Thank God. Look, I'll tell you all about it when I get there, but I wouldn't take on anyone new and I would screen old members, just to make sure they didn't get bitten lately. Say in the last month."

"Your word is gold, so I'll take it. You will explain,

though. See you tonight."

"You will."

Heading back to the office he had set up, Kasey clicked on Deke's frequency and got a reassuring click in return.

Which was when the squawk box from the Doc sounded. "Mr. Arlington! Please, you must help. Jason is loose in the compound. He... he attacked Lauren."

"Did he bite her?" How in the hell was he supposed to go hunt the compound with the sun shining bright outside? He'd forgotten his parasol.

"I don't think so." The old man drew in a sobbing breath. "Please."

"I'll call up surveillance. Deke will be here in minutes, and I can try to narrow down just where Jason is." Goddamn it, he hated sending Deke into something like this. "You lock down and take care of your girl. Did he just lose it, or what?"

"Yes. I was drawing blood."

"Christ. You didn't lock an animal like that down..."

"You can yell at me later. Please find him."

"Yeah, yeah." Kasey hung up with the Doc and pinged Deke. "We got a situation, lover."

"Now what? I'm five minutes out."

"The primary is running loose in the Doc's facility."

"Are you locked down?"

"I am now." The door locks hissed shut even as Kasey keyed up the cameras and heat sensors and shit. "I swear, I don't get how he controlled this place with one rent a cop locked in here. I'll try to pinpoint his location. You might have to take him out."

"If I have to, I will. I'm almost there, baby."

He sure as hell hoped so, because from the looks of things, Jason was on a tear. More than one camera showed chaos in the compound, with whole rooms torn to shreds. Jason was looking for something.

Kasey just hoped it wasn't him.

Deke squealed into the compound, the gates closing behind him quick enough that he didn't think anyone could get out. He'd leave the two sleeping beauties in the van, since they hadn't so much as twitched, and he figured with the alarm on, they were just as safe there as anywhere.

Making sure he had enough ammo to kill an elephant, Deke rolled out of the van and keyed his throat mic. "Where am I going, baby?"

"Start with the commissary. He's looking to build his strength, I bet. You know how ravenous you get."

"The moon is days away, baby." The full moon did make a wolf hungry, Deke knew that for sure. "Where the hell is the back-up the Doc promised would be here?"

"I don't think this guy goes by the moon, and don't count on it. Sundown soon, so if you want to wait…"

"No!" No, he wanted this over and he didn't want Kasey anywhere near this freak. God knew what tainted werewolf DNA would do to a vamp. "Just follow the destruction, huh?"

"Yeah."

Deke nodded, tuning out Kasey for the moment, sharpening all of his senses to try and catch a hint of his prey. Once he entered the buildings, it wasn't hard to follow the trail, but the damned fool wasn't anywhere near the food.

"You armed, baby?"

"Yeah. He's heading this way, isn't he?"

"Yep. Stay put. Hold tight. I'll be there in a few."

"Holding."

Goddamn, why had they agreed to do this? Oh, right. The money. They could fucking live at the Rose for a month off of this job. If they lived through it.

By the time he reached the wing housing the security office, Deke was raring for a fight. Fucking assholes, messing with a genetic code that had been in place for fucking ever, making his life fucking miserable because he was a sucker for a wolf in trouble, even if she was a lying bitch...

He slammed through the double doors leading into the corridor that housed Kasey's little cubby, watching Jason rip doors off hinges, all decked out in full moon form. Well, except for the parts that were invisible.

Fucking A, that had to suck.

Deke fired a warning shot over Jason's head. "This isn't helping you get better, asshole! Back off!"

The big head turned, razor sharp teeth bared. "Kill me."

Backpedaling, Deke stared, his gun hand never wavering. "What?"

Jason roared, the sound bouncing crazily off the walls. "Kill me!"

Oh, Jeez. That was why Jason was going for Kasey. The guy knew Kase would have the cojones the Doc and Lauren didn't. Kasey would've killed the poor bastard on sight.

"Come on, man. They can fix you. I promise."

"Bullshit." The deep laugh sounded like a howl. "I'll kill him. I'll kill all of you. I can't control it." Jason's whole body bowed, the transparent parts filling in, bulging as Jason grew even bigger, claws reaching out for him.

God. Deke hesitated that half a second too long, long enough for Jason to leap at him, teeth dripping with saliva. He rolled out of the way, out of the reach of those snapping jaws, coming up ready to fire, ready to wound.

Just as he squeezed the trigger, another shot rang out, and blood and gore splattered Deke's chest. Bits of bone pelted him, and Deke cursed, blinking away the nasty shit on his face to stare at Kasey, who stood in the doorway of the security room. Kasey held a big old gun that fired armor piercing rounds.

"Only way to make sure is to take off the head, right?"

"Yeah, baby. I was going to try to…"

"I know. Try to save him. Pack and all that shit. You and your wolf law." Kasey shook his head and smile, the look positively evil. "You know what the vampire rule is, right?"

"What's that?" Deke stood, wiping off more gunk.

"Kill them before they can kill you."

Before he could even laugh, the sound of running feet had him spinning, pointing his weapon at the unguarded hallway. He lowered it when he saw Lauren and her father, the old man panting hard and almost blue.

"Oh. Oh, Jason." Lauren came to look down at the body, her face creased in what looked to be real sorrow. "I'm sorry."

"Shee-it." When all of them stared at him, Deke shrugged. "Hell of a time to be sorry. You got two more out in the van, Doc. I suggest you start thinking about how to cure them instead of worrying about your little girl."

Lauren opened her mouth, and Deke stopped her, holding up his hand. "And you, missy. You might think about just sucking it up and admitting you are what you are. It ain't such a bad life. Put on your big girl panties and deal with it. Without me or Kasey, here. We quit."

The old man stared down his nose at Deke, sniffing. "Is that the best advice you can give?"

Deke looked over at Kasey, who shared a smile with him. "Hell, no. That's the werewolf code."

"Hey, you two. Enjoying your night?" Jonny stepped right up to the couch he and Deke shared, running a hand down Deke's back. Kasey felt the shiver that ran down Deke's spine, couldn't miss it the way Deke was all over him like a cheap suit.

Jonny had great hands.

"Yeah," Kasey said, smiling up at the big guy. "You did us up right, buddy."

"Good, good. Thanks for the heads up on the donors."

"No problem." As it turned out, the people Jason had bitten hadn't infected anyone else, but as a big part of Jonny's business was setting up werewolves as vampire feeders, it never hurt to be too careful. "We were just about to head to our room, if you wanted to join us."

"Mmm. Thanks for the offer." Jonny leaned down to kiss Deke, then him in turn, the heat in the room seeming to turn up ten notches. "Got a meeting in five, though. I shall have to take a rain check."

"We'll hold you to that," Deke said, his voice a low growl. They both loved to play with Jonny. The man didn't play nice at all.

"Later." They both watched Jonny's ass until the man was out of sight.

"Come on, baby. Let's go find some privacy." Deke crawled off his lap, holding out a hand to help him up.

"Good idea." Kasey took that hand and hauled himself up, pulling Deke close as a second skin. "Hungry."

"Yeah?" Tilting his head back, Deke offered up his throat, that tanned skin pure perfection. "We could put on a show right here. I'm easy."

"I know. Love that about you." His fangs scraped that fine skin for a moment, opening a tiny cut that he could lick a trickle of blood from. "But I want just you this time."

"Then let's go." All but dragging him, Deke pulled him along, taking him to the posh private room that Jonny had assigned them. They tumbled down on the big bed, tearing at each other's clothes, both of them needing.

Kasey had planned a slow seduction. They'd had wine out in the club, and Kasey had fed Deke all sorts of finger foods, leading up to slow kisses and lingering touches. They'd celebrated surviving their damned job, not being like poor damned Jason.

The whole slow thing went out the window as soon as they were naked. Well, the figurative window. There were no real ones in their room at the club.

They rolled, Kasey landing on top, his legs straddling Deke's hips, and Kasey struck hard and fast, sinking his fangs into Deke's throat. The hot, strong flavor of Deke's blood flowed into him, sliding over his tongue, making him moan.

Deke bowed under him, body tight as a drum, muscles tight and hard. Something else was hard, too, prodding against his ass, and Kasey didn't even think. He just rose up and pushed back, reaching behind him to guide Deke home.

That hard cock slid right into him, thick and scratchy and so good he wanted to scream with it. He might have screamed, but it was muffled against Deke's skin, drowned by the flood of coppery liquid Deke gave up to him so easily.

They rocked together, Deke pushing up into him, his own hips pushing down. His prick rubbed against the soft skin and rough hair of Deke's belly, the friction almost enough, but not quite. Deke felt like an iron rod in his ass, so hard, so good, and Kasey rode for all he was worth, hands clutching at Deke's shoulders.

"Harder, baby. Again. Bite me again."

Nodding, moaning, Kasey moved a few inches and bit down again, finding a new flow of life, feeling Deke's elation in every heartbeat.

Christ, nothing had ever been this good. Not in all his years.

They moved faster and faster, Deke's hand finally snaking between them, finding his cock and rubbing hard, pulling at him. Demanding.

His body arched, his hips snapping, and Kasey licked at the holes in Deke's skin, getting every last drop he could before they closed up, before he sat up and took Deke as deep as he could, his ass slamming down against those lean hips.

Deke's eyes glowed golden for him, those big, rough hands both pulling at his cock now, and Deke started talking, started begging.

"Baby. Come on. Oh, Christ. Need you so bad. Need to come. Need to taste you. Please. Just a little."

Oh. Oh, God. Deke rarely asked, didn't push him to share his blood often. Kasey nodded, raising one hand to his neck and cutting into his skin with a sharp nail, leaning down so the first drop fell right into Deke's open mouth.

Deke howled for him, pulling him down and sealing hot lips over the cut, sucking hard. Inside him, Deke's cock pumped and jerked, filling him hard and deep, really giving him everything.

Kasey moaned, his prick full to bursting, and when Deke bit him hard, asking for more of him, Kasey gave it. He came like a load of bricks, his come coating their bellies, the very last drops of his blood falling into Deke's mouth, his wound closing up.

Collapsing down against Deke's chest, Kasey chuckled. "You know, I had this whole plan…"

"Blame Jonny," Deke murmured. "He's always raising the stakes. Asshole has a knack."

"Uh-huh. I blame the Doc and Lauren, actually. I'm damned glad we're alive and unscathed."

"You and me both, baby." Deke kissed his mouth, loving on him, licking a drop of blood from the corner of his lips. "You and me both. What have we learned from this experience?"

"Never to take a job from a tall, cool blonde?"

Deke laughed, reaching up to tangle hard fingers in his hair, pulling him down until his mouth was inches from Deke's. "You got it. Even if they are werewolves."

Kasey chuckled, taking a hard kiss before nodding. "*Especially* if they're werewolves. Your code be damned."

"I can live with that. Kiss me, baby."

Smiling, he pressed his lips to Deke's, letting the kiss get them all revved up again. He could definitely live with that.

Belling the Cat

The club was running itself. The customers were happy, drinks were flowing as hard as the blood, and the smell of sex filled the air. Ah, a regular night at the Bloodrose.

Jonny smiled, watching Duke, his floor manager, smooth out some sort of dispute over a sweet little wolf and his contracted partners: two vampires, both possessive and toothy. Pretty.

Really, these days he wondered why he even came to work. He had made himself obsolete. Sighing, he shook off the ridiculous idea that someone as old as he would indulge in feeling sorry for himself. Especially since he had perhaps fifteen hours of work waiting for him. Obsolete, indeed.

He unlocked his office but didn't bother to turn on the light, sinking down into his cushy chair and debating whether he wanted to order a glass of the house red. He took a deep breath and... blinked. Something was askew.

Something that he should have noticed when he walked in, for a fact. The window was not closed entirely, which he never did, simply because sunlight could be deadly to someone like him.

Jonny stilled, listening hard. Life. He could hear a heartbeat.

Well, perhaps he should have turned on the light. His eyes adjusted with preternatural speed; a thief's eyes may not do so well. He moved with all of the speed he could muster, turning on his desk lamp.

A black blur streaked across the floor, heading toward the window, so quickly that he barely focused on it. Jonny leaped for it at the last minute, only his fancy metal blinds keeping the... whatever it was from getting away. His hand caught in heavy, plush fur, pulling.

The snarl was low, deep, the threat clear.

Oh. No, indeed. He did not think so. Jonny snarled right back, shaking the animal by the ruff.

Huge and sleek, black as pitch, the cat's huge paw batted at the blinds, fighting to tear them down.

"Damn you, stop that." Yanking mightily, Jonny sent them both flying back against the opposite wall, far from the windows. The heavy body landed fully against him, a lashing tail battering his legs.

What a magnificent creature. And... yes. It was male. Exceedingly male. Sort of... amazingly male.

The cat stilled, growling, trembling in his hands. He could feel the heavy, corded muscles, drawing up to spring.

"No." He said it clearly, sharply, knowing that somewhere the animal might win out over the man inside that cat.

The huge head swiveled on its neck, bright green eyes fastening on him with a glittering mix of aggravation and curiosity.

"Show me what you took." He knew it, now, knew that this big kitty was there to steal something from his collection. Or his safe.

The green eyes went wide in a patently obvious 'who me?' look.

"Mmm. Yes, so sweet. Nothing at all wrong with you being in my office. Looking for a club application?" That heavy body felt so warm.

The cat yawned, showing huge white teeth.

"I wonder what you look like as a man." He had drugs. If he could get to them, he might find out.

That tail thumped again, then the cat rolled away, flopping off his legs.

"Now, now." He sprinted to the window, blocking the way. "Give back what you took, and you may go."

The cat huffed, grumped, and crouched.

Keeping himself between the cat and the windows, Jonny scanned the room, his eyes flicking over everything. The safe. The wall panel was out, but the safe was still closed. Whatever it was he wanted, kitty hadn't gotten it.

And kitty didn't look too pleased about it, either.

Smiling, Jonny stepped aside. "You can go now, my dear."

The rowl was frustrated, that tail lashing furiously before the cat leapt, big body twisting, slipping out the window and into the night. Obviously, Jonny had something Mr. Kitty wanted. The cat would return. And if he didn't, well... Jonny smiled. That cat had a pheromone signature that would last for days.

The night had just gotten a lot more interesting.

Chapter Two

Luc watched the sun as it began to sink.

Ten minutes.

He had ten minutes

He stripped off quickly, stashing his clothes in a plastic bag inside another plastic bag inside a canvas backpack behind a dumpster. It only took a few seconds to shift, his body eager to be fuzzy, to be stronger.

Eight minutes.

Sticking to the shadows, he leapt from landing to landing, heading for the window he'd breached two nights ago. Mic had been... less than pleased to hear he hadn't retrieved the files. His jaw still ached a bit from the reminder that no one crossed Mic Salvia and lived.

No one.

Seven minutes 'til sundown.

Hurry.

It would take him two minutes to open the safe.

The windows were reinforced, but the very outside edges were caulked poorly, so it took no time to slide inside. The room was dark, cool, and he was alone. He made it to the safe and shifted back to man, needing his fingers. Five minutes.

Come on.

Come on.

The safe was in the same place, the little thing not very strong. Not very secure.

Very empty.

God damn it.

He told himself, very firmly, that he could panic later, after he was gone. After he was heading out of town. Luc went to the big desk, hunting, nostrils flaring. The files on Salvia's employer had to be here.

Had to.

Two minutes.

Fuck.

There was nothing. Even the sleek laptop was gone.

He was a dead man.

Okay.

Okay. Out. Home. Grab the stash and the car and run. Rio.

Rio was nice this time of year.

He thought of fur and fangs, claws and tail, muscles jerking and shifting.

The Rolodex caught his eye just about the time he finished changing. Someone had to have a home address. Right?

He hopped up on the desk, took the Rolodex in his mouth and hit the window.

Hopefully, he wouldn't get it too wet to read, but it was one of those fancy things with a lid. Ridiculous vampire of luxury.

He slid out the window as the sun set. Maybe he wasn't dead.

Not yet.

Chapter Three

Jonny sat back on his leather couch, his robe wrapped firmly around him, a glass of wine and blood in one hand. He was waiting for the show to start. In fact, as soon as the sun had gone down, he'd unlatched his metal blinds. Leaving a gap big enough for a cat.

The air in his office had been rife with panic and fear and a healthy dose of pure testosterone.

Lovely. Intriguing. Sometimes he was just so... bored. So, now he waited. Here, kitty kitty.

The cat waited almost an hour outside the window before daring to slip in, pitch black and sleek as midnight. His couch was not situated to watch the sunset, so he was fairly well hidden from the cat, but he could tell the moment the cat smelled him and knew it wasn't just residual scent.

The soft touch of claw to wood stopped and the air went charged. Electric.

Jonny didn't move this time, didn't turn on a light. He just watched. Waited.

The unmistakable energy of a shift tickled the base of his throat, and the beautiful sleek cat turned into a lean, tanned man with the greenest eyes he'd ever seen. Green eyes and a rather breathtaking array of fresh bruises.

"I need a file. One file. How much?"

"Did you get in trouble, kitty?" That made sense.

Persistence like that meant someone was pushing.

"You could say that. How much?"

"How much for what?" He sipped his wine, admiring the man's form.

"I'm supposed to get a file for Mr. Jim Black." Like that could be a real name. Fuck.

"Ah." Sitting back, Jonny crossed one foot over the opposite knee. "Why would you want that?"

"How much?" He could see the man's pulse beat from where he sat.

"I don't want money." It surprised him, that it even came out of his mouth. He normally held on to his business files with an iron fist. One never knew when he would need dirt on someone powerful, and the man in the file had... interesting tastes and an obvious issue with telling the truth.

"What do you want? I have resources."

Jonny tilted his head, giving that the consideration it deserved. "I think you have what comes naturally, and that it what I want."

"What?" He saw the nostrils flare, knew the cat was scenting him, the air.

"I'm not sure if you're aware of the nature of my business." He paused, waiting for the bare nod that came. "I have never found someone I wished to make a contract with. I want you."

"Me?" The word was honestly confused.

"Yes." That surprised him as well, the simple, bald shock. "I want six weeks."

"Six weeks. And I get the file first?"

"You can have it tonight." Jonny knew that was taking a chance, but he had to believe that obligation would bring his cat burglar back at least once. After that, he knew he could hold someone's interest.

The man's head tilted. "I have one condition."

"What's that?" His cock twitched, but Jonny willed it down, not wanting his cat to smell anything afoot.

"If I don't come back tomorrow, someone makes Mic Silvia pay."

"That is a condition I can eagerly meet." Absolutely.

Those green eyes stared at him. "Six weeks. One file."

"And all I need is your nights." That surely didn't seem so bad.

"Agreed."

All this, and he didn't even know Mr. Kitty's name. Impressive.

"Good." Standing, Jonny crossed the room in a flash, holding out his hand to shake.

Up close, the bruising was worse, the scent of male pheromones better. There was life, right there, right beneath that smooth skin. Jonny licked his lips. He owed the man a file first. He was a vampire of his word, after all. "Come."

The bare feet didn't make a single sound on the wood floors.

He led the way to the safe, silently retrieving the file. When his cat would have reached for it, Jonny pulled back. "Tell me your name."

"Luc. I know yours."

"I suppose you would." He handed over the file. "I don't have an electronic back up." He knew where most of the information could be compiled again. He didn't need one.

"I don't really care, to be honest. This is enough to keep me alive."

"Meet me one half hour after sundown at the Bloodrose. Tomorrow. If you prefer not to come in the front, you're conversant with my office, hmm?" For a tiny moment, Jonny couldn't resist the urge to touch that smooth skin.

He trailed his fingers down one arm, just as he would pet a cat.

Warm. Incredibly warm, that skin fascinated his fingers.

Yes. Impulsive or not, he had made the right choice. Jonny stepped back, hand dropping to his side.

"I'll be there." Luc rolled the file up, hand coming up with a rubber band from his desk in a move so fast he barely saw it. Then the file was secured and the man rippled, shifting more rapidly than he had ever seen. The cat was huge, those lovely eyes staring at him.

"I shall count on it." Jonny watched the sleek creature leap out the window, excitement thrumming through him for the first time in... well, since he'd met a certain werewolf who was not his to take.

Chapter Four

Fool.

He was a fool.

Luc slipped into the office at the Bloodrose, paws padding as he carefully sat his bag of clothing down. Still, he was a live fool, which had been seriously in question a couple of days ago. The vamp wasn't in here, so he settled, cleaning his paws, his face.

The door slammed open, the light springing on to blind him. "Damn it, Duke. I don't care who you have to piss off, move the schedule around. I want that private room."

He jerked back, sliding into the shadows out of pure instinct.

The door slammed behind the vamp, who was alone, just on the phone. Those pale eyes scanned the room, searching.

He panted, fur standing up on end as he watched.

Those eyes finally focused on him, and Luc saw the pupils dilate, the flow of words hitching a moment. "No... Yes. Thank you. 'Night."

His nostrils twitched and he searched for the vampire's scent. Spicy. Somehow it shouldn't smell that good. Right? There should be the scent of... disease. Something.

Death.

His head tilted, his tail twitching. Interesting. He

drew in a deep breath, rolling the flavors of the air on his tongue.

Jonny. His name was Jonny. Jonny came forward, one hand reaching out to scratch behind his ears. Normally he would bite that hand, but... Oh. There.

Right there.

His eyes crossed.

Long, strong fingers dug into his fur, knowing exactly where to stroke, where to scratch. His claws rolled out into the rug, his instincts taking the pleasure, wanting it.

"No one touches you, do they, Luc Kitty? I imagine you're starved for it." Almost contemplative, that voice, that touch. Slow, steady. Perfect.

He stood for the scritches as long as he could before his nerves and his pride made him slink away, tail high, twitching at the tip.

"Would you like something to eat? A drink?"

He yowled softly, exploring more thoroughly. This place had so many interesting sparkly things. Jonny let him go for quite a while. Let him wander. Then the man came and stood in front of him. He rumbled, stretched, then rubbed his cheek against the bulge in the man's slacks, scenting Jonny.

"Oh. Well, now. That's a very fine start." Jonny reached for him again, fingers sliding over his cheeks.

He nipped a bit, testing the vampire's fingers. Tasty.

"No eating. Licking and biting yes." The man stroked his ears one more time.

He growled softly, showing his teeth. He didn't take orders.

Really.

He nibbled again, then leapt onto the vamp's very large, very smooth desk. "Yowl."

"As charming as this is, I need you to be a man for the things I have planned." Standing back, Jonny folded his arms.

He stretched, considering sharpening his claws. He was much safer like this.

"Not on my desk, you don't." Maybe he was a little too obvious.

There were always the drapes.

Or the upholstered chair or...

Oh, look.

Sparklies.

He reached out, fascinated by the shine.

This time Jonny caught him, long fingers wrapping around his leg, just above his paw. "Now, if you please. We have a contract."

Forcing himself into human form was always more challenging. Always. He almost envied the dogboys. They were so much... closer to human.

"I... I came here." He stretched, slipped out of the vamp's fingers.

"You did." Now it seemed Jonny watched him even more warily, calculating his next move.

His clothes were in the bag and he went for them, smoothing his hair back as he moved.

"There's no need. A robe will be provided for you, if you like."

That had him bristling again. More orders.

"I brought clothes." He crouched down, unzipping his bag. Soft clothes. Silky clothes.

Why did Jonny keep staring at him?

"Yes, but you will not need them." Now Jonny was frowning, the short blond hair artfully arranged. Or maybe not. Maybe vamps were just... perfectly touseled. It was possible. "I would swear you said you understood the nature of my club."

"I..." He stopped, smoothed his hair again, refusing to stutter. "I understand."

"Oh. Well, then." Somehow it made him feel better

to see Jonny smooth the crease on one pants leg, flick an invisible bit of lint off one sleeve. "A robe, then? Perhaps a drink?"

"Please." He was feeling very bare and in desperate need of his tail. "This is... awkward. Is it always like this?"

"Generally? Yes, it is when the principals don't know one another." The man finally unbent enough to smile, showing an impressive set of needle-like teeth.

"It makes me want to clean my whiskers." He stepped forward, eyes on those teeth. "Have you bitten many people?"

"Define many." One hand slid down his arm, fingers closing around his wrist. "For my age, probably not. I can be... remarkably discerning."

Luc stilled, vibrated. He wasn't used to being trapped.

"You really must get used to being touched, Luc." But Jonny let go of him, moved to hand him a robe made of a silky material.

The fabric had him purring happily, sliding the robe around him. The touch was cool, then warmed quickly, the cloth clinging to his skin.

"Better?" That smile made him relax even more. It was far less toothy.

"Mmm." He nodded, stretched. "Thank you. It's lovely. What do you want from me?" His eye was caught by the light under the door, feet passing by.

"I think tonight I simply want you to sit, have a drink, and we'll have a chat." The smile widened. "You're like, as they say, a cat in a room full of rocking chairs."

"My tail's been at risk for a bit. Makes one jittery." He approved of that smile, somehow. "I'm not like this." He motioned to his furless, de-clawed self. "Often."

"No? What a shame. You're quite beautiful either

way." The slow appraisal that accompanied the words made him feel naked again.

The way his cheeks heated made him rumble softly, shift his weight to the balls of his feet. "Where do we sit?"

"What would you like to drink? And I intend to go to the sitting room."

"Kahlua and cream?"

"Absolutely." Jonny rang what had to be the bar, ordering drinks, and then pointed him toward a nearly hidden door that concealed a very comfortable room.

He grinned; he'd wanted to explore that door and what lay behind it. There was a soft chair, wide and overstuffed, that he contemplated for a moment, but he had a feeling Jonny would want to share a seat. The large sectional sofa looked just as good. He headed toward it, curling in the corner, feet tucked behind him.

"Good choice."

A discreet knock on another door, one he hadn't seen, sounded only moments later. He could smell cream, along with the coffee scent of Kahlua and something delicious. Some kind of snack, hidden under a silver dome, and it would have made his whiskers twitch if he had them.

He had no idea what he was expected to do, so he waited and wondered, nostrils flaring.

Jonny took the wheeled tray from the unseen waiter and brought it over, settling next to him. "I took the liberty of ordering some seared ahi tuna and some beef carpaccio."

"Oh..." He could purr. He honestly could. Purr and rub and... Oh. Fuzzy. Breathe, Luc. "It smells heavenly."

"It does, doesn't it? I might share the carpaccio." One hand slid over to lie on his thigh, warm and easy. Not creepy at all.

His muscles jerked and he reached for the Kaluha,

telling himself to breathe. No one wanted to cage him, right?

"You are very uncomfortable. Is it me, or is it simply that you're unused to being with people?" Those fingers dug in a little, massaging his leg.

"Three days ago they were threatening to hollow out my teeth and take my balls. Twelve days ago I was..." Well, maybe telling a near-stranger that he'd been raiding a jewelry store for a particularly perfect pair of emeralds wasn't the best idea, but still. "Working. Today I'm drinking cream and smelling tuna. It's not you."

"Ah. Well, then. Indulge in the tuna. I have no interest in taking your balls. I might want to use them a bit." One finger crept dangerously close to said balls.

He yowled in a gentle warning, the cream sliding on his tongue.

"Hmm? Is the drink not to your liking?" That smooth voice held a distinct note of amusement.

"Don't laugh at me. I bite."

"Do you? So do I." Moving a fraction of an inch closer, Jonny bumped hips with him.

"Does it hurt?" He couldn't resist the urge to ask.

"Would you like to find out first hand?" The whole feeling in the room changed, becoming charged, Jonny leaning toward him.

He rumbled and leaned away, then back. Did he want to know? Yes. Did he want to find out? Maybe. Very definitely maybe with a side of maybe not.

"Are you sure?" One hand landed on his belly now, way too warm for a vamp, and Jonny's mouth hovered just over his throat. "Well, then, perhaps it's something we should explore." Smooth lips pressed to the skin of his throat, Jonny's fingers stroking through the thin robe.

Oh. Oh, that was odd. His instincts warred—lift his chin, bite, roll, growl, something.

Then Jonny's fingers slid around and drew a circle in the small of his back and every nerve he had fired and he arched. Scratching lightly, Jonny drove him crazy, making him want to claw at the couch. This low sound tore out of him, and his chin lifted, the whole room spinning.

"Mmm. Yes, I thought that would get you. Such a kitty." Was that supposed to be a bad thing?

"Not all of us can be tail-chasers."

"Or wind-up teeth, hmm?" The warm puff of Jonny's laughter left a damp spot on his neck.

"Chomp, chomp, chomp." The idea amused him, had him chuffing with laughter.

"What a lovely sound." The man was pushing him and yet not, that hand working the spot that would be just above where his tail would be.

His body was caught, hips arched, everything attuned to that spot, that touch.

"So hot. I can feel it just under your skin. That hot, magical blood." The words moved against his skin, each one pressing against him.

His toes curled, his fingers wanted their claws. His heart thrummed, pounded like it was trying to get out, which was a gross thought, honestly. Who wanted their heart to do that?

Not even zombies.

"Let me taste it, Luc. Let me taste you." Jonny's fingers pushed against his back, and the tiniest prick of teeth stung his throat.

"Taste." The word came out as a long, hissed purr.

"Yes." The fangs sank into his skin so easily. Everyone described it as a needle. It was more like a hot knife through butter. All he felt was the pull.

Swaying with it, Luc purred. That sound turned into an all-too-human cry as the fingers on his spine dug in.

Then Jonny moved, those teeth slamming down into

his skin, and the pull became a huge thing, everything in him flowing into Jonny, his cock hard as stone. Eyes wide, he humped, hips dragging his prick over skin, over silk, everything inside him screaming for release.

"So hot." Jonny murmured it against his skin, pulling free. Then the man kissed him, fangs pricking his lip.

He fought to hold onto his humanity, to hold onto his need.

"Luc. Now." The demand was plain, but it matched what he wanted. Matched his desire. Seed sprayed from him, and he yowled, nerves firing, pleasure suffusing him.

"Oh, yes. That was lovely." That mouth. It moved over his skin until Jonny could lick the bite mark on Luc's throat.

The lights seemed to swing, sway, back and forth, sparkling in his eyes. Those long fingers undid the silk robe, Jonny rubbing the come into Luc's skin. "You smell delicious."

The purrs rumbled out of him, one after another, the cat right behind his skin.

"Let him come," Jonny murmured, settling back against the couch.

His muscles rippled, the cat leaping to the fore before he could even offer his thanks. He stretched and purred, head-butting the vampire happily, the smell of sex and blood luscious.

Pushing the empty robe away, Jonny stood, hand on his ruff. "Shall we move to a room with a bed? I shall bring the food."

He pushed his nose against Jonny's balls, breathing in the rich, male scent. Beds. Beds meant pillows. Sheets. Comforters.

"Oh, now." Jonny laughed, the sound genuinely pleased. "Come along."

He licked once, then stretched, waiting for Jonny to lead the way. They made their way through the back door that the waiter had come in, through a private corridor. It was comforting rather than insulting, that Jonny didn't drag him through the club.

This place smelled interesting and he explored as he walked, sniffing and looking, peering through doors. There were all manner of men and not men. Vampires, wolves. There were many he could not identify by scent.

By the time they entered a room with a huge, soft bed, his whiskers were vibrating, his fur standing on end. The room had a tiny lingering odor of disinfectant, but it wasn't unpleasant, and the fine cotton sheets were very clean.

He stuck his head under the pillows, exploring, batting them before settling.

Jonny laughed out loud and slapped his butt. "You like it, yes?"

He spun around, taking Jonny's wrist between his teeth, holding carefully. No swatting. Jonny's eyes widened, and the smell of arousal suddenly overpowered the scent of cleaner. Completely.

He growled softly, letting it sink into a purr, his tongue tasting Jonny's skin.

"Now, now. Don't bite too hard. I bite back."

He knew.

He thought he might approve.

He shook his head a little.

"I had such plans for us tonight." Laughing a little, Jonny pushed at him until he sprawled, paws up and batting at the ceiling. "I suppose I was a bit ambitious."

He wasn't sure what that meant, but Jonny stripped, sat down and he rolled, cheek sliding on one thigh.

"Very soft." The muscles under his cheek twitched, like his touch tickled.

He nuzzled, pushing closer to the male scent of the delicate, soft balls.

"Mmm." The sound was almost like his purr, low and rumbly and happy.

He licked, testing the skin there, the flavor sure and sharp, male, but somehow dark.

"This is... I'm not at all sure that's a good idea."

He snorted. Silly man. Then he licked again.

Moaning, Jonny rocked back and forth, pressing against him a bit. The man's body certainly seemed to think it was a good idea. His tongue dragged up along the heavy shaft, moving to the delicate skin over the tip.

"Rough." Breath hitching, Jonny humped up, hands pushing against the bed sheets.

He growled, slowly letting the cat go, letting himself stretch out long, become soft-skinned and human.

"Oh..." That was even more like a purr. The sound was completely different to human ears, almost subvocal.

He licked again, this time lapping at the tip of Jonny's cock, playfully.

"That's it." Now Jonny's hands were on him, sliding over his shoulders.

His shoulders curled, rolled, sliding against those hands. Fingers slid into his hair, Jonny holding him, thumbs rubbing his cheeks. Then the man guided him down, trying to get more of the surprisingly thick cock into his mouth.

Luc pulled back, growling softly. "Careful." He wasn't sure about this... about the touching.

"Very well." Jonny lay back on the bed, robe open, letting him look his fill. "I shall let you touch me first."

That eased him, and he leaned forward, hands and mouth on the smooth skin, lips tracing the thick, heavy cock. Jonny stretched, muscle sliding smoothly under pale skin. It was almost catlike. Luc could appreciate that. He bit at one muscle before settling, focusing on the flavor at the tip of Jonny's prick.

He could almost hear Jonny's hands creak, clenching, wanting to touch him. The man was as good as his word, though, letting him have his way.

"Mmm." His tongue was fascinated, sliding over the slit in Jonny's prick, over and over.

"Luc. Your tongue. Rough." That wasn't a complaint. Not by a long shot.

He chuckled, pointed his tongue and pushed the tip in, tasting the bitter and salt. The skin under his tongue felt hot, smooth. The taste was deeper than most men. Richer. Earthy.

Good.

Jonny tasted good.

He rumbled happily, licking harder, wanting more.

"More." Jonny echoed his thoughts, pushing up, opening his mouth.

Deep, happy sounds rumbled out of him and his fingers rolled, pushing into the sheets as his tongue worked Jonny's prick. The world narrowed, his entire focus becoming bed and Jonny, sheets and skin. It felt decadent. Right. He started purring, letting the vibrations move around the hard cock spreading his lips.

Jonny pumped those hips up, pushing and pushing, need in every line of every muscle.

Luc reached up, dragged his nails along the length of Jonny's chest, scoring the skin, ever so lightly.

"Luc!" Jonny liked that, too. The man was very open to pleasure. It was heady.

Chuffing happily, Luc took Jonny down to the root, swallowing hard around the tip of the man's cock.

"Yes. Oh." The moan seemed to echo deep, right under his cheek.

He scratched again, demanding, needing to know that

flavor. Slick drops of need slid out over his tongue, telling him how close Jonny was. Telling him that vampires weren't that different from men. Or cats.

He dared to slip his fingers behind Jonny's balls, fingers sliding around the tight little hole. Jonny's hole went tight, resisting him, but those balls drew up hard and fast. Every muscle quivered, Jonny grunting for him.

He tapped and growled and sucked, all at once. Come. Come. He wanted to know.

Jonny gave Luc what he wanted, growling for him, hands scrabbling at the bed. The taste was nothing short of amazing. The urge to lick and lap and taste took him, his tongue searching for every drop.

By the time he was done, Jonny was limp, panting, the sound odd. Like it was unnecessary but unavoidable.

Luc purred softly, nuzzling the flat belly, the scent of the tuna beginning to be as tempting as the man.

Jonny laughed. "You're hungry."

"Mmmhmm..." He bit a little, purring deep in his chest. "And there's tuna."

"The best kind." One long-fingered hand settled over his heart, as if feeling the vibrations. "I will spoil you rotten."

He wasn't sure how to feel about that, so he didn't bother. He nuzzled against the curve of Jonny's elbow, testing his teeth there. "Will you? Will I let you?"

"I think you will." Jonny's other hand slid down his back, nails scratching hard.

His spine arched, immediately, his fingers and toes curling.

"Mmm. I think you might let me do anything, if I asked the right way. Eventually."

"Nonsense." He didn't follow orders. At all. Luc nibbled up along Jonny's arm, tasting.

"Is that a wager?"

He tilted his head. Oh, that could be deliciously fun. "Absolutely."

"Oh, good. I love a little spice in my games, hmm?" Jonny bent, nipping hard at his shoulder.

His hips rolled and he pounced in response, yowling happily. His vampire laughed, biting him again, making his skin draw up in goose bumps. This might be the best bet he'd ever made.

Especially if there were sparkly things and tuna involved.

Chapter Five

Jonny woke alone.

He was used to that, as generally only when Kasey and Deke were feeling generous did he wake pressed against a firm, muscled body.

Too bad, in this case, however. He'd been looking forward to seeing if Luc woke as a man or a cat. He would bet on the cat. He sat up, eyes caught by a huge black rope dangling from the top of his wardrobe.

No.

Not a rope.

Not a rope at all.

Well now. Someone liked to sleep in high places. Jonny chuckled, going to get the fly swatter a patron had given him last year. The ridiculous thing had a diamond in the handle base.

Luc was comfortably perched, the tail the only thing moving. Beautiful, Luc was simply beautiful.

Absolutely a stunning animal.

Jonny grinned, feeling his fangs prick his lips. Then he swatted that tail with the swatter. Hard.

"Yowl!" The explosion of motion was stunning, the swatter bashed out of his hands as tail disappeared, clawed paw appeared and a snarl filled the air.

Grumpy kitty.

He dodged easily, laughing like a loon. "Here, kitty, kitty."

Luc answered him with a low growl that turned questioning as Luc licked the poor, affronted tail.

"Come down, hmm? It's still night. That means it is my time."

Luc arched, tail flicking, then leapt to the bed, landing with a thud on the mattress.

"Much better." Jonny smiled, stroking the offended tail.

The tip of said tail flicked and twitched, Luc staring at him, watching every motion he made. Jonny rolled to his back, baring his belly, enticing Luc to play. He scratched right under Luc's chin, too. Luc stretched, rocking into the touch for a long moment before the heavy body toppled over, right on top of him, whiskers tickling.

"Oof." Laughing, he dug his fingers into the fine, thick fur. It was like having a lover and a pet.

Loud purrs vibrated along his body, the sound echoing inside him. It made everything in him sit up and take notice. It was ridiculous how this... creature affected him. A rough tongue landed on his chest, scraping up along his skin.

"Now, now. No licking unless you're willing to follow through as a man." One had to draw a line somewhere.

Those eyes twinkled at him, challenged him. Then Luc licked again.

Laughing, Jonny pushed the heavy head away. "No. No biting, either."

A soft growl answered him, Luc nipping. Those teeth were almost as sharp as his. Almost. Luc's whiskers dragged over his arm, paws batting him playfully.

"Bad kitty." Really, none of this should be arousing.

Luc spun, that rough tongue dragging viciously across the tip of his cock. Jonny moaned, his whole body arching, bucking. That felt insanely naughty, which was silly. He'd seen and done it all, hadn't he?

Then the lick came again, and again, and he thought perhaps he'd missed one more lovely act. This was something that might ruin him for life, in fact. And he planned on a long, long life.

Luc's heavy head landed on his stomach, tongue catching each drop of liquid need that poured from him. He stroked Luc's ears, the urge to laugh when they twitched surprising him. Those bright eyes met his, the face shifting just the barest bit, like the human couldn't quite overtake the cat.

"Come on, sweet. You can do it. I want to touch all of you."

Luc pushed that broad, flat face into his hands, the muscles twitching and jerking, the man trying for him.

"Yes. Yes, Luc. I can feel you." Look at that. That was hotter than anything else that had happened all evening.

The struggle made his prick ache, made him begin to burn with need, with a surprising hunger. Slowly the cat faded, the panting, bare naked man in its place.

"Well. Hello." He smiled, his hands still cupping Luc's cheeks, his thumbs rubbing over smooth skin now.

"Hello." Luc's eyelids went heavy, the soft panting sounds filling the air between them.

"So pretty. You really are a lovely creature. Cat or man." Jonny let his leg rise, the bottom half sliding up between Luc's legs.

Luc arched, a low purr rumbling through him. "I'm not human often."

"No? Well, you are sensual and lovely, either way." He could see more possibility for biting without the fur, however.

"Thank you. You smell good." Luc's hands measured his hips, his waist, then moved up to touch his chest.

"So do you." Leaning into the touches, Jonny licked a trail along the side of Luc's neck. "You taste good, as well."

The simple touch had Luc vibrating, shifting against him.

"Mmm. I think you might be more hungry than I am." That was saying something. Jonny wanted to bite. Now.

"I ate tuna. It was luscious."

"For this, I mean." He let his fangs scrape the fine skin just over Luc's pulse-point.

"Biting." Luc growled softly, the sound fascinating, oddly confused. "No biting."

"No? I think you like it." He knew Luc liked it. That had been graphically pointed out to him.

"No."

He licked again and Luc arched against him, the scent of need most overwhelming.

Then Jonny gave in to the urge and bit, needing the hot pump of Luc's heart.

The rush of power was overwhelming, energy and heat flooding him. His eyes rolled back, and Jonny clutched at Luc's skin, drawing the man in, tasting the wildness of the cat. So good. He'd never tasted someone so... feline, so close to the edge. It was heady, addictive.

They rocked together to the beat of Luc's heart, which never stuttered, never slowed. It was... Jonny had never... Luc yowled softly, seed spraying against his belly without so much as a touch.

Moaning, Jonny drank for a few more heartbeats, his body bucking, his balls emptying with little ceremony. Really, it was extraordinary.

Soft purrs eased him down, Luc's face lax and still, the lovely eyes heavy-lidded.

"Oh. Thank you." He stroked Luc's cheek, knowing the cat would come back soon. Of course, so would the dawn, and his Luc's obligation to him would be over for the time being.

Luc purred for him again, louder this time, the soft

cheek sliding against his paw. "You. You are different."

"Am I?" He'd like to think so, but he wasn't sure what he was being compared with.

"Mmm." His wrist was given a quick little nip.

His skin tingled, just from that tiny touch. "Now, now. No biting."

"That was my line." Luc's laughter tickled his skin.

"It was, hmm? I think you like it too much to say no." That suited him. He got something of a high from drinking Luc in.

"Should I come back tomorrow night? Will the window be open?" Luc's cheek slid against his, scenting him.

"It will. I'll be waiting." Jonny chuckled. "I have a feeling you'll be bad for business."

"Always." Those beautiful eyes laughed at him. "Always."

Chapter Six

Luc paced below the window, back and forth, over and over. He'd been starving when he got home and had slept the day away.

Now he was back.

Curious and questioning and hungry.

A sound from behind startled him and he leapt, bouncing from sill to sill to reach the one he needed.

The window in question was open. As promised.

He slid inside, his instincts keeping him in the shadows, his whiskers vibrating. He could hear Jonny moving around, humming a little. It made him want to yowl. He crouched down, butt in the air, readying to pounce.

The humming stopped abruptly, and he cocked his head, listening. Oh, his man was coming. Wait... His vampire?

He vibrated, waiting for the right time.

The right time came when Jonny's shadow fell across the windowsill. Perfect.

Luc pounced, twisting in the air to attack. Jonny sprang forward to meet him, grabbing him around the middle and spinning to toss him toward the desk in the center of the room. He landed on his feet, panting, tail twitching. Play!

Crouching, Jonny made a come on motion, taunting him. Oh, so fast.

Luc ducked his head, sliding to the floor and staying

low in the shadows, watching as he circled.

Neither of them made a move for long moments. Jonny didn't make any sound when he breathed. If he breathed.

Luc's tail twitched, his whiskers vibrating. It was time.

Now.

No.

Now.

No.

Now.

Yes!

He rushed Jonny, going for the low shoulder-butt.

Jonny went down under his attack, obviously expecting him to come in high. Sometimes sleeping on armoires had its advantages.

He nibbled on Jonny's knees, then pounced the round butt with both front paws. Tag.

Up and after him as soon as he bounced off, Jonny caught up quickly, hand on his tail. He slid away, pushed up on his hind legs, batting at Jonny playfully. Laughing, Jonny bared his fangs, slapping at Luc's paws. Such strength. No man had ever had the strength to play with him.

He wrapped his arms around Jonny's neck, rubbing their cheeks together in a warm greeting before bouncing down and back again.

They played for what seemed like moments, but had to be nearly an hour. Finally Jonny just tackled him, rolling them across the floor so they slid into the wall.

He hugged Jonny tight, licked Jonny's jaw from chin to ear.

"Oh! Scratchy." That laughter made him happy, deep inside.

He nuzzled in again, then let the human out, trusting

Jonny with it. "Evening."

"Good evening. I hope you don't mind. I ordered the fish."

"I like fish." He plucked at Jonny's fancy shirt. "You have clothes on."

"I do. You don't." Chuckling, Jonny pulled off his clothes, tossing them aside. "There are robes, when we decide to move to the private room."

"Mmm." He purred and slid downward, mouth open on the soft belly, teeth scraping gently.

"Good kitty." Long fingers curled into his hair, helping his motions along.

He growled softly, warning that he wasn't to be trifled with. Then he lapped at Jonny's navel. The skin there was thin, pale, smooth as anything could be. He nudged Jonny over onto his back, exploring with his mouth and fingers, butt swaying in the air. Stretching long, Jonny let him have everything, neck and chest, belly and cock.

A rap came to the door, and the sound had him springing back, growling low. "Boss? There's someone here asking to see you."

"Shit." Jonny sighed, rolling to his feet. "Sorry, sweet. I shall return, hmm?"

Gathering his clothes, Jonny dressed quickly and slipped out of the room, leaving him with the barest squeeze on his shoulder.

He sighed, shifting back to his natural form to explore. There were so many shiny things, on shelves and in boxes and on the huge desk. He gnawed on the leather chair for a while, then opened the safe, just to practice.

By the time the door opened again, there was a pile of letter openers, cuff links and pinky rings on the desk. The light came on, making him blink and growl. He slipped under the desk, peering out at the intruder.

"Luc? Where have you... Good god." Jonny broke off,

staring about. "Well, you did find my silver ring, hmm?"

He chuffed, tail sliding on the floor. He found many things.

"I have not seen it for two years." Jonny lowered his voice conspiratorially. "To tell the truth, I thought Kasey stole it."

The thought of another thief in his territory made his ruff puffy. Jonny's was his to rob.

"We were at the same club at the same time, back in... Well. You don't wish to know how old I am, hmm?" Smiling, Jonny came to him, extending a hand.

He slipped out, wrapping around Jonny's legs, tail held high.

"You did eat my chair, however. For that, you might owe me a forfeit."

He tilted his head, yowled. Eat was a very strong word. He preferred... nibbled.

"Yes, eaten. Look how it will poke my bum." Every so often Jonny said something that reminded Luc that he just wasn't from the States. It was... cute.

He pounced the chair seat, paws landing with a thud.

"Yes, well, I do not have your fur carpet." The teasing made his tail twist happily, made his whiskers vibrate.

He headbutted Jonny, then stretched, muscles rippling.

"You're utterly repentant, I can tell." Those long fingers pushed through his fur, scratching hard.

Totally. Completely. Oh, there.

He arched. Right there.

"So pretty. I swear, you make me forget myself. I had such plans." He could smell Jonny, could tell what the man wanted.

He nosed Jonny's balls through the heavy slacks.

"Forward cat." But Jonny was rubbing against him, hips rocking slowly.

His paw landed on one thigh, claws just barely threatening.

"Are you threatening me, Luc?" One brow rose, Jonny's eyes seeming to glow a moment.

He considered that, but truly, what choice did he have? He rumbled deep and pushed. Jonny smiled, slow and delighted. Then the man jumped him, wrestling him to the floor. He yowled, batting and twisting, letting Jonny feel his strength. He could tell that Jonny was impressed, maybe proud, and the tussle got more serious when Jonny stopped holding back. Yes. Yes. Real play.

They slammed into furniture, bashing around together and crashing into the door, then back, Jonny coming to rest atop him. Jonny's eyes glowed, the light in them so bright for him. Happy. It was good. He slapped Jonny with his tail, right across the ass, chuffing happily.

"Now, how is that fair?" Strong fingers dug into his fur, scratching him nice and hard.

Oh.

Oh.

His head fell back and his throat worked, pure pleasure in his muscles, his fur.

Good.

He felt the touches all the way down to the tip of his tail. His body rolled, trying to get more. His claws pushed out, released, and he twisted. More.

"Don't you scratch my floors." Jonny laughed breathlessly, tickling and teasing before settling in to scratch again.

He tried to focus on fighting, on playing, but all he knew was a wild, restless joy.

"Come to me as a man, my cat. I'm beginning to have a terrible need." Jonny was hard for him, and those eyes... Jonny was going to eat him alive.

Luc chuffed softly, imagining himself bare and long,

like a man. Like Jonny. The change was slow, but steady, coming to him.

"Beautiful. I love to watch you change. So different from..."

A little stab of jealousy hit him. He yowled softly and swatted. Different from who?

"I have a friend who is a wolf," Jonny explained, stroking his side. "It looks so painful for him."

He stretched, let himself become even more human. It was less painful than awkward for him.

"You're just so sleek. So lovely." Now Jonny was licking at his lips, leaning to kiss him.

"Jonny." He purred, his entire body vibrating.

"Yes. Luc." The kiss went deep and a little toothy, blood welling up along his lower lip.

He opened up, hands dragging down Jonny's back.

Wanted.

He wanted.

Jonny moaned for him, starting to rock a little, and that felt right, the slide of cool skin along his, a little slick with his sweat. Their cocks knocked together, then dragged, sensation rocketing up his spine.

"Oh." The small sound pressed against his skin. Jonny rocked against him, gasping.

"More." He leaned up, teeth on Jonny's shoulder, testing, teasing.

"More," Jonny agreed, licking at him, biting at his chin, his throat, leaving tiny stings.

His hands landed on Jonny's ass, sparks sliding up his spine as they grounds together.

"Harder." He wasn't the only one who needed more, who wanted this so badly.

"Yes." One of his feet braced against the floor, letting his hips slam up.

Their skin slid together, the friction undeniable, the

need trembling right on the edge. All they needed was... was something. He growled, fingers digging into Jonny's ass, and he bit Jonny's shoulders. Those lean legs came up to wrap around him, holding him closer. The scent of them together drove Luc crazy.

"I need." Luc couldn't think, couldn't breathe, could only ask.

"Yes. I do, too. I want inside you, Luc."

The words made his stomach go taut, his muscles singing as his cock throbbed. "In."

They could posture later, when his balls ached less.

"Thank God." Jonny ought to be thanking him, but he would point that out later, when Jonny's cock wasn't pressing against his hole.

Bearing down, Luc took the head in, let it scrape and stretch him. The burn had him shivering, his muscles bunching and releasing in unfamiliar ways. There were advantages to being human, though.

Human skin was so much more sensitive.

It worked for him because Jonny's hand was everywhere, sliding over his chest, tugging the curls above his cock, pinching his nipples. It was perfect. Well, he thought it was perfect. Then Jonny bit into the flesh of his shoulder.

His cry echoed, his ass clenching around Jonny's cock.

"Mmm." The moan seemed to make the fangs stuck in his skin vibrate, a sensation at once disturbing and amazing. Jonny bit a tiny bit deeper, his hand smacking against Luc's ass.

The world seemed to stop, to be nothing but heat and blood and need. Good. Good. Please. Drinking deep, Jonny slammed into him, opening him up, sending him soaring. Flying. Luc spun out of control, held close only by the teeth and cock piercing him.

It went on and on until he wanted to scream and claw at the sky. Then Jonny snapped against him, hips moving in short bursts, hot come filling him up. Luc grabbed his prick, tugging once, twice, the pulls almost vicious, but exactly what he needed to drive himself over the edge. When he came, Jonny's fangs sank deep into his skin and muscle, making everything in him fire like lightning.

The whole world had turned red.

They eased back down to the... floor? Desk? He didn't remember if they had even made it to the settee. It didn't matter. All he could feel was Jonny. Shuddering, he held on, hoping that Jonny would help him, would bring him back.

Stroking his back, Jonny helped him down, let him float down slowly. His purrs slid out of him, vibrating his chest.

"My pretty cat. Thank you." Sometimes his man seemed oddly formal, reminding Luc that he was from another age.

He nuzzled in, rumbling his thanks, his pleasure. "Smell good."

"Yes. We do." Jonny smiled, patting his butt. The phone rang not two seconds later, making him jump. "Damn."

"Busy busy." He suspected Jonny was too busy for a lover, even for six days, much less six weeks.

"I just need to make sure people know I'm occupied." Easing away, Jonny headed for the phone, back to him, ass tight and inviting.

He slipped back into his natural form and stretched, before leaping from floor to chair to bookcase. Jonny pulled on a robe and settled into a chair, tapping away at a sleek little laptop. Luc would have time for a nap.

He cleaned his tail and whiskers, then settled. Yes. A nice nap.

Chapter Seven

"No, no. I don't care how much he's offered. I told him he was no longer eligible for club membership." Jonny typed as fast as his fingers would go, looking up the vamp who had applied for membership at Bloodrose. Again.

"Honestly, you would think we were the only club that catered to... Well, we are, aren't we? Poor fellow." Actually, it gave Jonny great pleasure to turn the asshole down. A patron like that could ruin a whole business.

"I'll let him know, sir." Duke's low growl made him smile. The wolf was a grand assistant, barring the periodic worthless evenings every month, and was preternaturally efficient. Must have been the whole pack alpha instinct.

"Thank you. Anything else?"

"Would you require a private room tonight, sir?"

"I would like one, yes, if we have one available. Let Annabelle know I will be unavailable for a bit."

"Yes, sir. Have a good evening."

"Thank you, Duke." The idea of introducing Duke to Luc made him smile.

The phone line went dead, leaving him in the quiet luxury of his office. He turned, searching for Luc, finding a kernel of panic in his belly when the man was nowhere to be seen. He took a deep breath, the scent of musk sudden. Ah. His Luc.

Jonny turned, finding the slippery beast atop the

cabinet, tail dangling. He'd been there before, hadn't he? Grinning, Jonny plucked a rubber band out of his desk drawer. Luc's tail was moving, slowly, lazily. Carefully taking aim, Jonny sent the heavy band winging toward Luc, aiming for high up. That was where the tail was stable enough to be a target. Right before it hit, Luc's tail snapped out of the way. Then bright green eyes stared down at him, challenging.

Oh, ho. Someone wanted to play. And they said werewolves were difficult. Jonny swiveled his chair, putting his back to Luc. He'd never met a were who was so... invested in his animal side, so curious. So...

Oof.

Luc landed on the desk in front of him, paws on his shoulders. Smiling, he rubbed noses with Luc, hands coming up to stroke the huge paws. So soft. Luc's purr vibrated through him, loud enough to tickle somehow.

He waited until Luc's eyes were half closed with pleasure, until the big cat was totally relaxed. Then he ducked under those long legs and ran, heading down the private hallway to the room Duke would have arranged by now. He could feel the cat moving behind him, could feel the unfamiliar sensation of being hunted instead of hunter.

It sent a little thrill up his spine. Such a lovely game. He almost purred himself. He felt a paw swack his ass, painless, but firm, pushing him faster. An extra burst of speed sent him shooting into the dark room, where he leaped over the bed and landed on the other side. Jonny slipped off his robe and crouched in the gloom, waiting.

He could see those eyes, glowing softly, a pure green searching for him. Going very still, he tested his cat's hunting skills, loving the little shivery feeling that ran up his spine. He'd grown bored over the years. Jaded. Luc took that feeling away.

He saw Luc blink, once, then the eyes were gone, leaving only inky blackness. There was no sound, except the hypnotic thump of Luc's heart. That sound moved, but in the darkness it was disorienting. Jonny was used to being able to see. He saw the faintest outline of black shift to his right, then a soft thump as the mattress dipped.

As stealthy as he could be, Jonny moved to the end of the bed, ready to leap. Could he take Luc off guard?

Luc went still and Jonny imagined he could hear the big ears twitching. Good thing he didn't have to breathe. Oh, he could, and did. Jonny quite enjoyed all the things that came with air. Like talking. For now, though, he was glad he could still even that.

One paw swiped out, reaching for him, just missing. Oh, Luc was good! Jonny sprang up, reaching for those scoop-like ears. They flickered in his fingers, Luc yowling as he was pounced.

Laughing like an idiot, Jonny tore about the room, wondering what his staff would think if they saw him playing. Luc's paws batted at him, painlessly; the big cat chuffed and snarled behind him. He turned suddenly, catching Luc in mid air before flinging him to one side. Luc landed on his feet, snarled softly, then crouched down.

"Come on, kitty. Come get me."

That heavy tail thudded on the floor and then, bang! Fur and fang and claw and rough, hot tongue. They tumbled to the bed, Jonny grunting, rolling, scrambling against the slippery sheets. Luc was strong, hot, and fast. Teeth grazed his shoulder, Luc fighting to stay on top. His fingers dug in on either side of the bed, and Jonny lifted up, tossing Luc off. The smell of his blood bloomed. Luc tearing his skin deliciously.

Luc snarled softly, lapping at his skin, tasting him carefully. Moaning, Jonny wiggled, the feeling sending little shocks all over him. The tongue on his skin was rough, the tingles shooting down his spine. Smiling, he moved again, as if he was trying to get away. Just to see what Luc would do. Heavy paws wrapped around his waist, claws barely threatening. The message was incredibly clear. Stay.

Oh, that made him laugh, right out loud. Picky kitty.

Luc cleaned his shoulder, lapping at it gently until the flow of blood stopped, then the grooming and purring started, Luc holding him down with one huge paw. It was the oddest sensation, being cared for that way. It wasn't human affection at all. It was all cat. Luc rolled him over, cleaning him intimately, leaving nowhere untouched. By the end he was boneless, left feeling adored.

Jonny stretched, loving how Luc had made him feel. Needing it, really. The heavy fur was silken and soft against his back. They just rocked together a little, like he was just a man with a pet cat. Except no housecat would make him feel what Luc did. Luc's tail tapped against his leg, and Luc's whiskers tickled his shoulder, the back of his neck.

He thought about having a bit of a nap, but that seemed wasteful, somehow. As if he would be losing time. About that time Luc's stomach growled—he had the unique sensation of feeling the sound rumbled against his lower back as well as hearing it.

"Hungry, my cat? I can have a feast sent. More fish? Perhaps chicken" It gave him a deep sense of satisfaction to provide for Luc, as Luc provided for him.

The growling shifted to a lovely, deep purr, Luc's cheeks rubbing his shoulder.

"Very well. I'm afraid you must let me up for that."

He was rolled again, his stomach given a lick before he was released to find Luc cleaning his own face.

"Greedy thing." Not that he minded. Jonny called the

kitchen. "I need chicken. Something simple but good. And whatever the fish is on the menu as well. No bones."

"Yes, sir." The little chirpy voice was almost irritating.

Almost.

Jonny dropped the phone back in the cradle, rolling his head on his neck. He'd have to find out from Duke who that was and tell him never to let her work the phone again.

The touch of very human hands on his shoulders shocked him, surprised him badly. Whirling, he leaped back, hands up defensively. Luc stumbled away with a snarl, leaping over the bed. Shifting in midair, it was as if the man disappeared. He'd never seen anything shift so easily, move so fluidly.

"Oh." Damn. Damn it all. "I'm sorry, Luc. You startled me. I thought someone else had invaded our space."

A low huff and growl expressed clearly what Luc thought of that idea.

"You have never been a man without me asking first." That seemed a reasonable thing to point out.

Luc slinked out from behind the bed, whiskers vibrating.

"Much better." He held out a hand. "Please. Let me make it up to you?"

Luc came to him, nudging his fingers and demanding a scratch. Jonny gave it, wondering what Luc would think of what some of his customers required. Oh, not of him, though he had indulged in their games once in awhile.

Luc slowly morphed into a man, still kneeling, staring at him. "You looked like your shoulders hurt."

"Did I?" He was stiff, certainly. Something about that little voice on the phone had made him furious. "Would you like to rub me?"

"You did." Luc moved behind him, hands sliding on

his shoulders, thumbs digging in.

"Mmm." Good. Yes, good. His head dropped forward, giving Luc more access.

"I like how you smell." Luc purred, the sound happy.

"Well, that's good. As strong as your sense of smell is, if you hated my scent it would all be over." He could stay there for, oh, millennia.

Strong thumbs pushed into the muscles of his back, forcing them to release their tension. He leaned forward, hands naturally falling to the desk to hold him up. Jonny spread his legs for balance, letting Luc care for him. Luc's hands explored him, as eagerly as that tongue had. It felt both erotic and luxurious, letting someone touch him like that, without thinking of anything else. Without trying to find the work angle in it.

"Pretty, pretty." Luc kept purring and rubbing, touching, constantly offering him more.

"I'm glad you like." He was very, very glad.

Those hands found his lower back, lips on his nape. Jonny moaned again, his body starting to undulate, his ass pushing back. More. That purr turned into a sweet growl, lips becoming teeth. Yes. That felt perfect. The sting made him want to shout.

Luc's cock was long, heavy, sliding along the crack of his ass, again and again. He would have given the man anything at the moment. Anything, if he would just use that amazing cock like it was meant to be used.

"I want." Luc's teeth grabbed his nape, shook him a little. "Let me in."

"In." Nodding, he offered, arching his back like the most practiced whore. He wanted, as well.

Luc growled softly, the slick tip of the long prick sliding hot against his hole before his cat pushed in, took him with one lazy push.

Electricity shot up his spine, making him grunt. "More.

Luc. Faster."

"Mor-r-r-r-re." He felt that purred word all along his spine.

"You're a cruel kitty, hmm?" Not that Luc wasn't giving him what he needed. That cock split him, pushed into him again and again.

The soft chuff was punctuated by one thrust after another. Fangs sinking into his lower lip, Jonny pushed back, slamming his ass against Luc. His balls felt heavy, full, and his cock might just explode. Teeth sank into his nape, holding on, Luc shaking him, just slightly.

An explosive moan left him, his whole body shaking. That... "No—No biting."

All that earned him was another shake, a growl, another deep, hard thrust. He laughed. Indeed, Luc took as well to that command as he did. Biting good. Luc shifted, cock finding his gland and lightning shot up his spine. Yes. Yes, so good.

Panting, Jonny hung his head, arms shaking where he held them both up. He... he was going to explode. Luc never touched his cock, just slammed into him, over and over, working his ass, driving him over the edge. Jonny couldn't remember the last time he'd come from being fucked. Maybe sometime in the century before last.

Luc purred softly, the thrusts becoming long and lazy, his cat taking time to orgasm, to let him feel every second. Shifting, Jonny pushed back harder, squeezing his muscles tight around Luc's cock. That was one advantage to being what he was. Excellent muscular control. That purr became a surprised yowl, Luc pushing in deep.

"Yes." Laughing, Jonny did it again. Then again.

"Jonny. Pretty. Pretty. Please." The thrust became wild, the feral sounds more so.

"Now, Luc." He put the command into his voice, into his body when he clamped down as hard as he could.

Heat filled him, Luc's cry deep and needy.

That was almost as good as drawing blood. Almost. That would come later, after he'd fed Luc well.

Chapter Eight

L uc woke up in his apartment, the sun pouring in, something... He smelled something. His nose twitched, but besides that he didn't move.

Who was there? Who was going to die?

The tiniest sounds rustled through the front room, almost like scurrying rodent. Except that mice were not men-sized. He slowly, slowly dragged his feet beneath him, setting himself up to attack. The hanging bed swayed, just a bit, and his claws dug in.

The sound of cloth scratching on wood came from just beyond the door. Someone was being very careless. He slid down to the floor, heading for the sound, claws bared. As soon as the door cracked open, he pounced, snarling.

He twisted in midair when a needle slammed into his rib muscles, piercing the skin and feeling like it scraped against bone. Cold, huge steel. Ice seemed to slide through his veins, even as rage heated him and he attacked the now-closed door. What had they done?

What was this?

He hit the floor, bare knees slamming into the hardwood.

Knees.

He groaned, fingers tearing the needle from him.

Fingers.

Knees.

The feline in him screamed, trying to claw out and it wouldn't come.

The sound of running feet was indistinct to his human ears, but the man was clearly running away from him. What could he do like this?

He found clothes, shoes, coat. Hat. Then he headed for the front door. There were people coming up the stairs, he could hear them. Fuck. Fuck. The world was beginning to get fuzzy, distant. Odd.

Luc ran for the window, racing for the fire escape. The Rose.

He'd go for the Rose.

Jonny would help him.

If he made it there before the world went black.

Jonny sat at his desk, feeling the sun beat on the building outside. Some days it was like that, even buried deep inside the Bloodrose. He rolled his head on his neck, glancing away from the computer.

Why he was so restless escaped him, but he was. As if he were waiting for something.

A rapping came to the door, "Sir? Sir, there's a bit of an..."

"Let me *see* him!" That roar was terribly familiar.

On his feet and at the door in a heartbeat, Jonny opened the panel to find a very naked, and very bedraggled, Luc. "What happened?"

"Help me." Luc fell onto the floor in front of him, a huge, vicious bruise on the tanned skin.

"Luc!" Waving off the attendant, Jonny hauled Luc the rest of the way into the room, needing to know they were safe so he could examine his cat.

Those bright eyes were dull, dazed, scared as they

stared at him. "Jonny."

"Luc, what happened. Talk to me." He knew that had to be hard, but it was the only option. He rolled Luc gently, finding the bruise and checking it carefully.

"My place. A needle. I can't change."

"You can't..." A hot flash of rage lit Jonny from within. "Someone attacked you?"

"Yes. Let me stay? They were coming." Luc's eyes were rolling, throat working furiously.

"Of course you may stay." There. The tip of the needle was still stuck in Luc's skin. "Let me have someone analyze this?"

Luc nodded, hand hot where it wrapped around his calf. "I can't change."

"It's a drug of some sort. Don't panic, sweet. It will wear off." He had to get the piece of syringe out to Kasey. Then he could help Luc.

Luc groaned, curled up into himself, knees to chest.

Jonny threw open the door and snarled for someone to get Duke. Anyone. Run. Now. Someone had attacked what was his. Someone was going to pay. Jonny snarled, kicking the door shut and bending to lift Luc in his arms.

His cat was feverish, muscles twitching and jerking under his hands.

Duke was at the door in seconds. "Sir?"

"I need this to go to Deke and Kasey. I need them to make it their top priority." Kasey was a fellow vampire, and a private investigator with access to a lab. "I need to know how to reverse it."

"Yes, sir. Right away. Is there anything else?"

"Medical supplies. Something for Luc to drink. Something with protein." Damn it all.

"Yes, sir." The man was preternaturally efficient.

Jonny was glad for it now. Glad Duke didn't have the

chirpy, irritating voice, too.

Luc's green eyes stared at him, begging him for answers.

"We'll know what it is soon, love." He stroked Luc's cheek, meeting those eyes sure and steady. "There's nothing in a drug that can damage you permanently."

Luc curled into him, cheek on his thigh, panting softly. "Did I wake you?"

"No, I was working." His hands touched every bit of Luc's skin, finding nothing else untoward.

"You work too much."

"Do I?" Smiling a little, Jonny pulled Luc back into his arms and lifted. "You need a bath."

"Water." Luc snorted softly.

"As a man, it has benefits." It would feel good on those bruises, on the sore muscles.

"I can't change." Luc nuzzled his jaw.

"We'll figure out what's wrong, I promise, hmm?" He nuzzled back, holding Luc close.

He headed them toward the bathroom, toward the huge, heady tub. He left the lights off, not needing them. The water came on hot and steamy under his hand, a single touch starting the jets when the tub was full. That would help. Luc tensed, until they were submerged, then the long, lean body relaxed.

"There. I told you that would be better." He smiled, stroking a hand down Luc's back.

Luc nodded, murmuring softly—nonsense about bothering him and aching and running.

"Shh. You are not a bother." Not a bother, and his and hurt, and Jonny wanted to kill something.

Luc's tongue slid over his collarbone, the soft touch obviously one of care and comfort instead of arousal. If his cat had been able to change, that tongue would have been rough and heavy, pushing against him. It made him angry all over again that someone would do this.

He could feel those poor muscles, jerking and shifting, trying to relax, trying to do something they weren't allowed to do. Eventually, though, the hot water and his hands eased Luc, let the man relax.

"That's it, love. That's it." Jonny murmured it against Luc's skin, trying not to break the rhythm of his touches.

The quiet kisses and licks continued, Luc trying to purr for him.

"My cat. What am I to do with you, hmm?" He knew what to do, but that might have to wait a bit.

"Let me stay for the day."

"You can stay as long as you need to, love. We're going to fix this, and find out who wants you so badly." And kill them. Jonny would tear them apart.

"People in my line of work gather enemies."

"Indeed. They do in mine, as well." He understood that. He would still rip them to ribbons and tie the pieces around tree limbs. He thought Luc might quite like to watch that.

He kissed Luc's cheek, just below his ear, and let them float. The jets buffeted them a little, pushing them about. Jonny felt it when Luc fell into a deep sleep, the long body melted against him.

Humming, he stood, water pouring off him, and took Luc to the bed. It was a good thing he'd given up living anywhere but the club. He had all the comforts. His cat curled up into him, shivering until he drew the blankets up around them.

Jonny cursed his lack of body heat and thought about calling for hot water bottles. The way Luc clung told him not to move, though, and he stayed right where he was.

There would be time for everything later, from finding out about the drug to killing those who had done this.

Now was for Luc to heal and sleep. Somehow that had become the most important thing.

Chapter Nine

Cold.

He was cold.

He was cold and his tail was missing.

Luc blinked awake, growling under his breath. He hated waking up as a human, had since he started the change way back when. It was unnatural.

Distracting.

Wrong.

Wait.

He moved his shoulder, growling at the ache there, deep in the muscle.

"Well, I suppose asking how you're feeling is a bad idea."

Jonny. Jonny was there. Not holding him, like he had been when they went to sleep, but sitting in a chair with his little laptop.

"Better. Naked. My tail's missing." He wrapped the blankets around himself.

"I know." Jonny looked up, smiled. "But you look better than you did, I assure you. Are you hungry?"

"I don't know. Probably." He rolled his shoulder again, thought of his claws, his tail, his long, sharp teeth.

Nothing.

Nothing at all.

"Stop." Jonny closed the laptop with a click. "It will come back. It's the drug."

"How long?" He didn't know if he could stop.

"I don't know. Kasey has narrowed it down to a certain drug family, but he's not sure of the dose or the strength of what you got."

"Oh." He stood up, pacing a bit. He needed to go find out where the assholes were and kill them. After they fixed him.

"Are you? Hungry?" Jonny stopped him by stepping in front of him, hands on his upper arms.

"No. I don't think so. I have to go. I have to find them and make right again."

Jonny's hands were hot.

"Not until you have your strength back." Those warm, strong hands pulled him back to the bed, and Jonny sat with him.

He growled low, frustration and fear building inside him. "I can't *change*."

"I know." Stroking his cheek, Jonny stared into his eyes. "I can help."

"How?" He was vibrating, every inch of him awake and alive and screaming in pure aggravation.

Leaning in, Jonny bit down on the flesh of his shoulder. Hard. It made him cry out, which felt... good.

His head fell back, his muscles screaming happily at the sensations. "More."

"Mmm." The strong fangs sank farther into his skin, and Jonny pinched his ass, hard enough to make him jump.

"M...more." His own teeth bared, snapping at the air.

A rough groan was the only answer, but before he could blink he was facedown on the bed, Jonny on top of him. Those teeth sank into him, over and over. He yowled, hips bucking up, a raw joy filling him up with each stinging bite. A burning pleasure filled him, shooting higher and hotter when Jonny's hand landed on the side of his hip in a ringing slap.

Luc forgot about changing; he simply felt, his confused body caught by his Jonny. The slaps and bites had him arching, growling, digging into the sheets with his fingers. He was warm, finally, white hot and needing.

"Please. Mate. Mate. I need. I need you." He screamed out his need, heedless of who might hear.

"Need what?" There was no triumph in Jonny's voice. His mate didn't want to hear him beg. No, he could tell that Jonny wanted to give him exactly what he needed.

"More. More." He pushed back with his hips, grinding back toward Jonny. "Take me. Let me come."

Make him hot.

"Yes." Licking at the throbbing bruises on his skin, Jonny pulled back at the hips, one hand sliding down his back. Those fingers prodded his ass, pushing him open.

Purrs rumbled out of him, his thighs parting and his back bowed.

"More." Pressing deeper, Jonny opened him, letting him feel it. It burned, but it gave him something to focus on. Something to believe in.

"Yes. More." His head bobbed, his skin heated, all through.

"Now, Luc." The fingers slid out and Jonny's cock pushed in, scraping all the way. It made him yowl.

Those strong arms wrapped around his chest, drew him close as the heavy cock pierced him. Jonny slammed into him, hips smacking his ass, making the skin sting. Then Jonny's fangs pushed into him again, too, drawing blood to the surface. He screamed out his pleasure, body moving, working Jonny's cock

Growling, Jonny moved him, made him take all he could and then some. The biting, the fucking, and the sudden hard blow to the side of his thigh overloaded him.

Spunk poured out of him, the orgasm making every nerve buzz and spark. Crying out, Jonny jerked behind him, filling him deep. The feeling made him complete for that one moment, made him forget that he had no tail, no ears.

Those arms stayed wrapped around him, kept him close and surrounded. Better.

So much better.

"We'll keep you safe, sweet. I promise."

He licked at Jonny's arm, wrist, almost purring. "Thank you."

"You're welcome." Relaxing against him, Jonny kissed his shoulder. "Anything for you, my cat."

Luc purred low, nodded, finding himself blinking slowly, the nap calling to him.

"Sleep now, love. I'll be here when you wake."

Luc nodded, letting himself drop away, trusting in his lover to protect him.

Soon he would eat the men who had done this to him. Until then, he would let Jonny ease the pain the way only he could.

Chapter Ten

Jonny paced, waiting for Kasey's call.

It shouldn't be taking this long, really. Kasey was usually the soul of efficiency. If nothing else, by now Kasey's partner Deke should have stopped by...

The phone rang, and Jonny snatched it up. "Did you find out what it was?"

"Like you thought. Looks like a massive dose of Cretaphin."

"Damn. So how long will it take?" Luc would be able to shift again, as soon as the drug worked out, but it was synthetic, specifically designed for just such events. Shifters generally took it voluntarily to keep from changing at inopportune times.

"My best guess? Three weeks to a month. He got a brutal dose."

"Shite. Fucking hell." Luc would go crazy. He would tear himself to pieces. He was already scratching at his arms, in his sleep. Jonny had seen it with Deke once, his friend going nuts after three days. "Anything else you can tell me?"

"Well, if I gave someone this dose, Boss, I would be intending to kill him. This was a high-dollar hit."

"Damn it all." Sighing, he rolled his head on his neck, glancing at Luc, who slept fitfully. "Thank you."

"Anytime. Keep him safe, boss, or show him the door, huh?"

"Yes." He hung up, knowing that now they had to find out who had done this and what they wanted. To kill or just maim?

When he looked back at Luc, those bright eyes were staring at him.

"Hello, sweet." He smiled, trying to bite back his worry.

"Jonny." Luc rubbed along the sheets, still staring. "What's wrong with me?"

"I was right. It was a drug. They overdosed you, however." Slowly, carefully, he made his way to Luc's side.

"It's not permanent?" There was pure, blind horror in Luc's eyes.

"No. It could last as long as a month, though." He knew that wouldn't help. but it was better than Luc dying.

"A month? No way. That's... days. There's a full moon between then and now." The panic was palpable.

"I know." It might just kill them both, keeping Luc busy.

Luc groaned, one hand sliding against his thigh.

"Mmm." Jonny encouraged the touches, moving closer, letting Luc take what he needed. Comfort. Reassurance.

Luc leaned down, cheek on his thigh, rubbing back and forth, over and over. "Is there an antidote?"

"Not that we've found." He paused, stroking Luc's ears. "The dose should have killed you."

Luc growled. "They sent someone to assure the job was done."

"Yes, but you got away." Thank the gods. Jonny couldn't imagine not having Luc, now that he'd been with him.

"I ran." Luc rubbed again, teeth testing his skin this time.

"It worked." Jonny shifted, his legs falling open, letting Luc have better access.

"It did. I can't survive a month like this, a moon like this."

"You will because I won't let you do otherwise." He might have to ask Deke to help him, however. Deke was a werewolf. He would understand.

Luc's chuckle was low, rough, husky. "I don't think you get a say in that, lovely."

"You don't think so?" He scratched lightly at Luc's back.

"I... Hrm?" Luc arched, butt shifting.

"I think I do have a say, sweet." His fingers dug in a bit harder.

"No..."

He chuckled as Luc's eyes crossed. "No?"

Human or cat, Luc seemed completely unable to resist a good scratch. "No." That pink tongue flicked out, Luc arching.

"Hmm. Well, then, I suppose I don't have to try to comfort you." Jonny pulled his fingers away.

That earned him a low, warning growl. Luc was surprisingly good at that, in his human form. Jonny laughed, feeling like Luc was far more there with him now than he had been. Sweet cat. His cat.

Luc's face pushed into his stomach, nudging against the fabric of his shirt. Jonny reached down and pulled the fabric out of the way. Really, if he didn't have a business to run, it would be much easier.

"You taste good." Luc groaned, licking and lapping, tongue dragging on his skin. "Touch me."

He groaned, struggling out of clothing, trying to get skin on skin. His nails scratched, his fingers pinched, offering Luc all the sensation he could stand.

Luc helped him, tearing at his slacks. "Mate."

The word burned like fire in his belly. Oh, fuck yes. The rest of his clothes fell in shreds, and he turned on Luc, pushing his cat down into the mattress, kissing Luc fiercely. Luc growled, the sound wild and, he thought, happy as it pushed into his lips. If he could make his cat happy, even when he couldn't change? Oh, that would mean the world to him.

When had Luc become his? Become more than a challenge, a dalliance? Perhaps from the very beginning.

Luc bit his bottom lip, tugged it. "Pay attention."

"I am," he murmured, smiling against Luc's mouth. "What do you want me to do?"

"I want you to touch me. It feels so wrong, being stuck like this. Cold."

"I know. I know, love." Though he didn't. Jonny honestly couldn't remember what it felt like to be human. He could touch, though, could feel smooth skin and hard muscle.

"No, you don't, but you make it better." Luc grinned for him, eyes sparkling with a hint of madness, for a moment.

"Good." All he could do was bite down on the nearest skin, give Luc something else to think about.

Luc answered him with a bite of his own, dull teeth scraping on his skin. It felt odd, not to have the cat right there, teetering on the edge of danger. Jonny pushed that thought aside. As odd as it was for him, it had to be worse for Luc. He heard Luc's aggravated half-growl, felt the frustration in the very air.

"Shh. I know what you need." He did. He could give it easily. Jonny rolled, pressing Luc down on his back, leaning close to push his fangs deep into one hip.

"Mate!" Luc's heels dug into the mattress, the scream gratifying.

Jonny drank deeply, needing the feel of Luc under him,

inside him, even if the power was oddly muted by the drug. He wanted to go tear someone limb from limb all over again.

Luc whimpered, fingers on his hair, petting him, hips moving in slow circles as he fed. His cheek nudged the hard cock, and Jonny reached up, wrapping his fingers around it. He gentled to a slow suction, taking tiny sips to prolong the meal. Soft little words poured down over him—rough-edged purrs and moans.

Chuffing much like Luc would, Jonny rose up and nipped the tip of Luc's cock. Gently. His sweet cat responded with a curious chirrup, but didn't tense, trusted him and his control. His tongue pushed into the slit, fucking it nice and hard. Oh, Luc tasted good. Sharp. Earthy.

He felt Luc moving, sliding and tugging at him, then that hungry mouth was at his crotch, seeking to return the favor. Jonny turned his hips, letting Luc suck him in. He went all the way down on Luc's cock, ready to pick up the pace. Luc was ravenous, mouth like a well of flames over his cock, the suction sweet and perfect.

Poor baby. Not that Jonny was above reaping the benefits of the need Luc had. He would wallow in it while he could. Then, when his cat was returned to him, he would rejoice.

Jonny sucked, licked, his hand coming up to cup the heavy balls, so warm and full for him. He heard the happy purr, then Luc pressed down toward his touch. More. He needed more. Jonny arched up, feeding Luc his cock. He pressed against Luc's balls with his hand, rubbing the whole sac in a slow circle.

Luc's purr vibrated around his skin, the suction growing stronger and stronger as Luc took him down to the root. They sucked and loved, both of them making these insane noises now, both of them moving hard enough to injure a less-hardy lover. Even human, Luc was not human. No, his Luc was unique. Special. Feline to the core.

His fingers pressed against the strip of skin behind Luc's balls, demanding more reaction. Nails scraped along his thighs in a clear, stinging answer. Jonny jerked, his ears ringing a little it felt so good. He let Luc feel his teeth again, a tiny prick of fang.

Long fingers pressed against his hole, even as Luc's throat jerked and squeezed about the tip of his prick. Jonny shot, shouting and bucking, his whole body feeling the shock of it. Luc undid him completely. Each and every purr vibrated around his cock, making each pulse of his orgasm seem somehow bigger. Jonny closed his eyes and sucked, hollowing his cheeks, his fingers pressing hard against sensitive skin. That was the last bit he needed to make it perfect.

Luc's hips rolled, the careful thrusts becoming random, rough. Jonny bit down, wanting Luc to scream for him. Wanting the fire. Blood and semen splashed over his tongue, Luc's wail loud enough to shake the foundations.

He reached for Luc's tail, looking for something solid in the spinning world, but of course, it wasn't there.

Goddamn it. They needed to fix that.

Chapter Eleven

Luc managed to stay in Jonny's rooms for ten days before he'd had enough. He waited until Jonny left to do whatever it was he did when he wasn't hiding a drugged cat in his rooms, then he slipped out the window and down onto the streets.

First, he'd head home, get his affairs in order, and then...

Well, if he could change, he'd start by hunting Mic Silvia's family and attacking there.

If he didn't get a cure or an answer, then he'd start with their enemies and work his way through the underbelly of town. Luc wasn't going to consider what he'd do if he managed all that, didn't get dead, and still couldn't shift.

It was like an itch in a place he couldn't scratch. It was maddening, making him want to tear off his human skin. That was a fine image.

He headed through the streets, feeling like every eye was looking for him. He swore he could feel people calculating the risk of robbing him, of attacking. Prickly heat rose up on the back of his neck. The growl bubbled up in his throat, low and threatening, and he wanted to slash his tail, more than anything.

"You know, if you don't want to get hauled off to the booby hatch, you should stop snarling at people."

"Huh?" He whirled around, fingers curling into claws.

The man behind him had shaggy blond hair and a rangy body. He smelled strongly of wolf. "Jonny told me to keep an eye out for you. Good thing, too. There are a lot of other folks looking for you."

"Who? Where?" He could deal with them now. "How do you know Jonny?"

"Oh, we're buds. Have been for awhile." The guy smiled a little. "Name's Deke."

"Luc." He'd heard Jonny mention Deke. "You don't have to keep following. I'm just going home."

"Uh-huh. Then where?" Deke jerked his head in the direction he'd been going, obviously not really there to stop him so much as protect him.

"I'm going to start killing people."

"Ah." Deke walked beside him, hands in his pockets. "I can help with that."

"Excellent." He slowed as they turned the corner to his place. "I'm in the big green building, third floor."

Were they there? Everywhere?

"Recon first?" Deke was easy to understand, easy to work with. Not bad for a stray dog.

Luc nodded, muscles screaming as they tried to shift, wanted to shift.

"Just hang on, man. It will get better."

How it could, he didn't know. "How? Have you done this? Is there a way to make it stop?" Maybe there was something Jonny didn't know.

"I was on a job. The guy I was after knew what I was, but I didn't know he did..." Deke shrugged. "I couldn't shift for two days, and it made me crazy. I can't imagine the dose you got. You should be dead."

"Yeah." He nodded, feeling like he needed to bite at the air.

"I hated it." Deke clapped him on the back, nodding to his building. "I'll circle west. Don't move in without me, okay? I'd have two vamps waiting to kick my ass if I lost you."

He chuffed softly. "Two? That's sort of overwhelming."

"You know it. Kasey and Jonny double teaming? Damn." Deke's smile was a lot wicked.

"Mmm. Jonny is mine now. My mate." He wanted that clear.

"I know. I can smell him all over you, man." The smile didn't falter, but it seemed more friendly than flirting now. "He's a biter."

Luc nodded. "I know. It's... good."

Very good.

Possibly extremely good.

"Yeah. I got a real thing for it when Kasey does it." Kasey. Yes. Jonny had mentioned this friend, as well.

"Does it scar, eventually?"

"If you want it to." Deke winked. "It's fucking hot."

"It's sort of mind-blowing, really. It makes my tail twitch."

"No shit." Deke moved close enough that Luc could smell him, how happy the thought made the wolf. "Makes mc hard as a rock."

"We should eat after we're done, compare notes." They were close now, about to split up.

"We should." He got a slow nod and a slow once over.

Luc preened, just a bit. He wasn't as striking as a human, but he was passable.

"Okay. I'll meet you back here. Keep your ass in one piece. I want to see that tail when it comes back."

He nodded once, then scooted toward his home, toward his things, toward...

He stopped, sniffed. There was something...

Something acrid.

No. No, they couldn't have burned his place. His den.

Someone would have...

Something hit him from one side, pushing him hard. He snarled and twisted, but the cat still wasn't there. Deke grabbed his arm, yanked him, and he took a few steps, trying to understand what the wolf was telling him.

"Bomb. Bomb. Run, man. Run!"

Bomb. He registered what that meant, his feet began to move, and before he could blink, the world went up in a ball of flame.

Chapter Twelve

Help me get him inside!"

Jonny heard the commotion, heard Deke's voice, even as his butt settled into his office chair. It sounded like quite an urgent thing. Jonny got back up and made for the door, a frown forming.

"What happened?"

"Oh, God."

"Deke?"

Well, that sounded... ominous.

Jonny threw the door open to find Deke standing there, Luc thrown over one shoulder, half a dozen club employees behind him. "Deke! What happened?"

His hands reached right out, relieving Deke of Luc's weight.

"What the Hell did your man *do*, Jonny? They blew it—the whole fucking building. The front door was set!" Deke's eyes were wild.

"I..." Luc was still, pale, but breathing. Jonny could hear his heartbeat. "Are you all right, Deke? You're bleeding."

"I don't know, man. What the fuck is this?"

"A mess." Jonny laid Luc out on the leather sofa, beginning to check vitals. "Let Duke clean you up?"

"Yeah. Yeah, I guess. I..." Deke shook his head. "My ears are ringing."

Jonny reached out, touching Deke's arm. "Please. Let

Duke make sure you're okay physically. Have Sandra call Kasey. Then we'll talk."

"Yeah. I guess."

Duke led Deke out, the big man still growling.

Jonny turned all of his attention to Luc, all of his senses. He needed Luc to be simply unconscious. Rather desperately.

The fine skin was peppered with tiny scratches, but the man's heartbeat was strong, pulse steady. There was no smell of internal bleeding, no sense of rapid decay as there would be with a bad injury. Maybe Luc's bell was simply rung. The bright eyes opened, the whites gone blood red.

"Luc?" Jonny didn't know where to touch, what to do or not to do. Luc might be in terrible pain.

"Jonny?"

"Luc. Can you hear me?" Poor Deke had said his ears were ringing. Maybe Luc's were, too.

"Yeah. Yeah." Luc blinked, blinked again, shook his head.

"Are you all right? Deke said they blew up your building?" Jonny watched his hands move on Luc's skin. They were shaking.

"Who did?" Luc's eyes dropped closed.

"I don't know. We're going to have to go, see what we can find." Giving up on being gentle, Jonny lifted Luc into his arms and sat.

Luc groaned, leaned into him, breath vibrating in a pseudo-purr.

"There. Oh, you scared me." God. He hadn't even known Luc was gone. Thank God he'd called Deke and Kasey in on the case.

"Mate." Luc rumbled, hands sliding over his arms, his back.

"Yes. Yes, my cat. No more wandering off."

"I wanted to gather my things, bring them home."

"Oh." Oh, he hadn't even thought. "Sweet. I'm sorry."

"Psht. It doesn't matter now."

Jonny couldn't imagine losing everything. Maybe that was the difference between cats and vampires. Of course, Luc could simply gather more... what did he call them? Sparkly things.

Jonny smiled, bending to kiss Luc's lower lip. "Do you hurt?"

"Not really." There was something, though.

"What is it, love? Tell me." He stroked Luc's arm, his ribs.

"You should check on your friend, huh?"

"Luc." He put a bit of a growl into his tone.

Those eyes opened up, stared at him, stared into him, the whites completely scarlet.

"I can't see."

It wasn't as awful as he'd thought it might be, being blind. Hell, it was easier than not shifting. It hurt less.

Luc explored the bumps and lumps of Jonny's couch, listening, waiting for the pacing and snapping and snarling to start again.

"I want to know everything about them, Kasey. I want to know who they are and where to find them, and how to hurt them. I am going to kill them all. Do you understand?" Yes. Jonny was way more upset than he was.

It was actually incredibly satisfying, to hear the rage.

"I understand." Kasey, who he had never met, had a British accent, and sounded amused.

Deke? Well, Deke was growly. It was pleasant.

Finally someone—Deke, from the smell of it—plopped down beside him. "So, who did you piss off, man?"

"Who didn't I piss off? That was, in effect, my business." He stole things—information, items, whathaveyou. It wasn't a warm fuzzy occupation.

"Well, you sure did it, man." Deke's hand felt good on his leg. Warm. "You need anything?"

"No. I think I'm okay. Are there any clues? Any at all?"

"I don't know. We're gonna have to do some sifting." Deke sighed. "I might be able to trace the scent of the guy who set the bomb. It was pretty clear."

Luc tried to figure out who would want him dead. Everyone he dealt with, for information, tended to hire him again. Surely it was someone recent, someone he didn't know well enough to know their motives. He listened to Jonny rage, idly flipping through his mental Rolodex.

"Jonny? What was in the paperwork you gave me?"

"Club records. Why?"

"Well, they were my last big job. What did you have on him?"

"I..." Jonny stopped, and Luc would swear he could hear fangs scraping against a lower lip. "He was conducting business in my club. Illegal business."

"Yeah? That could be a little bit problematic, Mate."

"Yes, well. I was only thinking of your health when I handed them over."

He chuffed softly, pleased. "Liar. You were thinking of your cock."

"Then my cock was focused on you, hmm?" Jonny moved close, his presence like a beacon.

He reached out, hands wrapping around Jonny's thighs. He could smell his mate, rich and powerful. Strong.

"You all right, sweet?" Jonny didn't move away,

muscles staying relaxed under his hands.

He could feel it, his true self, so close.

"Luc?" One of Jonny's hands ruffled his hair, fingers lingering on his temple.

He nodded, panting, his body screaming at him.

"Are you... Can you talk to me?" Now the worry was creeping into Jonny's voice.

"Mmmmmate." He growled, the change so close. So close. Please.

Please.

"Oh. Oh!" Jonny laughed, right out loud, reaching down to pinch his nipple. Hard.

He yowled, snapping at the air, body twisting. He could smell wolf, smell blood, smell his mate. His bones creaked, his joints changed, and he felt his tail. His tail! Finally. He leapt for his mate, his nose and whiskers leading him right where he needed to be. Jonny caught him, holding on, fingers digging into his fur. His fur. Oh, it felt good. Right.

His cheeks slid along Jonny's joining their scent as he vocalized, sharing his frustration, his joy, his *tail*.

"Yes. Yes, love. Oh, look at you." Jonny rubbed noses with him, holding his weight effortlessly.

He nipped at Jonny's ear, then licked along the strong jaw.

"He changed. Jonny, man. He shouldn't have been able to." He heard someone talking, but it didn't matter.

"Systemic shock. I imagine his body is trying to heal." They ended up on the sofa again, Jonny underneath him.

He ignored everything but the very important job of grooming and scenting his mate. Then he could nap.

Once he had a bit of sleep he could try to understand why he couldn't see. He had priorities, after all. Mates, naps. Then vengeance.

Chapter Thirteen

Jonny was going to rip someone's head off and shit down their neck. Well, not literally. He didn't do that anymore, really. But if he could, he would.

He watched Luc sleep, his hands constantly reaching for the long, black-furred body. It was amazing to see Luc as a cat again, but those poor eyes...

Deke and Kasey had gone, what little information Jonny had on the man who had hired Luc in their capable hands. They were detectives. Why not let them do the finding? Then the ripping and metaphorical pooping could commence.

Luc purred happily, pushed toward his touch, heavy tail swishing.

So much better blind and able to shift. It was stunning to him. Jonny smiled. Luc had called him Mate. Kasey and Deke had congratulated him well after Luc went to sleep, promising a real celebration later.

His cat rolled over onto his lap, heavy head on his thigh, paws stretching out. Kneading. Luc was kneading him in his sleep. Gracious. Thank goodness there were no claws popping out.

He reached down and started scratching, fingers digging into those poor abused muscles. Kasey had warned him that the changes would be less controllable for a few days, as Luc worked through the effects. It didn't matter. He was just so pleased that Luc could change, that his cat would not have to wait weeks to be, well, a cat.

Luc's eyes popped open, nose twitching madly.

"Shh. Shh. It's all right, love." He stroked Luc's ears, calming.

Luc yowled softly, head pushing into his touch, his cat panting heavily.

"I know, sweet. You just have to remember what happened. There was an explosion." He petted, talked, waiting for Luc to ease.

Luc slowly relaxed, face changing slowly, fur fading, then reappearing again.

"That's it, sweet. That's it. Kasey tells me the drug will make things unpredictable for now."

That earned him a nod, so Luc was with him, listening to him.

"They're out looking, love. They'll find out who I need to go and kill." Jonny still felt a jolt of icy cold rage in his chest every time he thought of that explosion. It could have taken both his mate and his best friend.

Luc bared his teeth, proving that he was right there, ready.

"Yes. Yes, you can help." Though if it was not simply flash-blindness, Jonny would never let Luc go on a rampage.

Luc chuffed, then stretched, muscles rippling, sliding under the pelt. Jonny smiled. Yes, things were much simpler to the cat than they were to the man. He stroked and scratched, letting himself sink into the simple physical touches. He found Luc soothed him, made it easy to forget the Rose for a moment, to forget his work.

That hadn't happened in a very long time. In fact, he couldn't remember the last time he'd thought of something as more important than the club.

Luc nibbled on his fingers, his wrist.

His elbow.

His upper arm.

"No biting." Really, wasn't it Luc who usually said that?

Luc chuffed, then bit his shoulder.

"Mmm. No. Only if you bite me as a man."

Luc growled softly, then shook him.

"Oh, bad kitty." Laughter took him, though, and he dug his fingers deep into Luc's fur.

Luc shifted again, lips on his ear, soft sounds leaving his lover.

"Mmm. Yes." He scratched and rubbed, loving how Luc responded to him. Loving Luc.

"Mate. I changed. I had my tail, my whiskers. You smell so good." His ear was nibbled. "Tell me we're going to destroy them all."

"We are. I promise." He'd given up vengeance a long time ago for himself. For his cat he would do a great deal.

"Yes." Luc nodded, wrapped around him, fingers moving randomly. "I like Deke."

"Do you? He's dear." Deke would sneer at that description, but the wolf and his vampire mate were Jonny's best friends. Possibly his only friends, really.

"Mmmhmm. He's solid. I'm ready for my eyes to work now."

"So am I, love. Do you..." He hated to ask, but he had to. "Do they feel as though they're healing?"

"They don't sting anymore."

"Oh, well." Was that good? Hell, he didn't know. Luc was still far closer to human than Jonny.

Luc's head tilted, nose twitching a bit. "You will not have to keep me, you know. I would not ask you to take a damaged mate."

"What?" When he worked out what Luc meant, he pinched that muscled ass. Pinched hard. "Stop that. I intend to keep you, one way or the other. You are mine, Luc."

"Yours?" Luc yelped, pushed him back onto the bed. "Are you sure?"

"I am. Very, very sure." He laughed, his hands all over that sweet body.

"Because I would want the best for you." Luc's actions did not match the words and those teeth scraped along his collarbone, marking him.

"You are the only one who has ever made me feel this way." He'd had a long life.

"Good." That single word had a wealth of satisfaction in it.

"It is." His hands followed the line of Luc's back, up and down. The feel of smooth skin and heat made him hum.

"You need to feed soon." Luc purred in response. "My skin feels tight."

"Do I?" The thought made his cock pull up strongly, his balls aching. "Are you sure you're up to it?"

Luc's answer was a sharp, strong bite on his shoulder, deep and bruising Well, that was... definitive. Suddenly he was ravenous, too. Jonny slipped to one side, bending to lick at the long line of Luc's neck. The vein there pumped steadily, throbbing under his lips, and he groaned at the promise under the thin skin.

The need slammed into him, the desire for the hot, metallic taste of life. Luc's blood was addiction made flesh. Jonny sank his fangs in deep, pushing past muscle to find a vein. The yowl rang out, echoing, the rich throb of blood on his tongue perfect, wild.

Sinking into it, Jonny sucked hard, drawing Luc into him. It was feral, a bright light in his head, coursing through his body. This was what he craved, his wild one, pouring into him, sustaining him. Jonny didn't know if he would ever be able to feed from anyone else again. This was too perfect.

Luc's fingers scraped down his belly, dragging on his shirt, snagging the fabric.

"Sweet." He murmured the word against Luc's throat, moving down a scant few inches to bite again.

This time the scratches were deeper, stronger, more claw than nail. Jonny moaned, his hips beginning to rock, his cock aching and hard, suddenly coming to his notice.

"Mate." Luc tore at his clothes, ripping at his slacks.

"Yes." His fangs slid free on the single word, and he shoved Luc down, struggling out of the remaining clothing. He needed skin. Now.

Luc was in constant motion, hands dragging over skin, those muscles jerking furiously. Jonny bit down again, teeth sinking into Luc's shoulder. God, yes. He didn't care if Luc never saw again. Well, he did, but this was his regardless. His.

His and he would defend it.

"Fuck me." Luc yowled softly, fingers tugging his hair, dragging him closer.

"Are you sure?" He had to ask, despite the hard evidence of Luc's need against him.

"Now." That wasn't a request. That was a clear demand.

"Love." Jonny held his fingers to Luc's mouth, making a silent demand of his own.

His lover opened up to him, sucking and pulling, tongue dragging on the tips of Jonny's fingers until he wanted to scream. He took it as long as he could before pulling away, sliding his hand down between the long, spread thighs. So open. So accepting.

"Hurry. I'll get fuzzy soon. It's close."

Hurry. Nodding, Jonny pushed his fingers inside that hot, tight hole, opening Luc quickly. The entire club would be hearing Luc's pleasure, hearing the happy, wild roar as he quickly stretched and touched.

He couldn't wait anymore. Jonny pulled free, his cock pushing in where his fingers had been. That body was like a heated fist, gasping his prick, drawing him in deep. Jonny paused, licking blood off Luc's shoulder, where it trickled down the pale skin. Fire there, too. So good.

"Mate. Hungry mate." Luc began to move, shift, driving himself down and up, again and again.

Moaning, Jonny grabbed Luc's hips and started to control the rhythm, knowing he needed to get on with it.

"I feel you. Harder." Demanding man.

"Harder," Jonny agreed, willing to give anything he could. He smacked the side of Luc's hip, slamming into that tight body, opening Luc unmercifully.

"Yes. Make me yours." Luc bared his teeth, snapping at the air.

Jonny did the only thing he could to make it better. He bit down one last time, pulling Luc into him while he pushed his cock into Luc's body. He tasted the rich blood as Luc came, the heat spreading between them.

Crying out, Jonny let go, his head falling back as his hips punched forward. Oh. His cat. Sharp claws dragged down his spine. Jonny was amazed that he didn't explode into tiny pieces. His body felt as though it wanted to, like he would just disintegrate.

Of course, he thought, perhaps, Luc would complain about that. Pieces of undead in the fur was... complicated.

Chuckling, Jonny came, his body bucking against Luc's. He was in such trouble with this one. Such wonderful trouble.

Long term trouble, he believed.

Chapter Fourteen

Luc sniffed, daring to slide out of the room he'd been in for so many days. There were so many smells. So many, but Jonny's was strong, so he followed it, whiskers to the ground.

There was a hallway, a corner that he hit his head on. Then there was smell after smell, too many, too much. He crouched, growling low, trying to ignore the panic that was crawling up his spine.

"Hey, Luc! What the heck are you doing out here?" He had to sift through his memories to find the voice, the cat not knowing it as well as the man. Deke.

He moved close to the voice, offering a yowl.

Deke scratched his ears, which made him focus, made much of the clutter in his head go away. "Man, you're a brave one, I'll give you that."

Of course he was, but mainly, he was bored. He'd explored the room, smelled. Now he wanted to explore more.

"Man, I'd be going nuts, I was you. You want to take a walk?"

He purred, pushed against Deke's hand with his head. He did.

"Come on." One hand stayed on him, Deke's fingers sinking into his ruff. "We'll go to the kitchen, get some grub."

He followed close, shoulder against Deke's knee. He

could hear the periodic gasps and noises, but they didn't matter. The smells here were fascinating. The closer they got to the kitchen, the more he smelled meat. Raw or cooked, red or white or fish. Oh.

He panted, his breath chuffing out of him, over and over.

"Yeah. Kind of amazing, huh? What do you want? I'll grab us some grub. Roast chicken?" Deke was fun, not talking down to him at all.

He bobbed his head. Chicken.

"Yeah. We get boneless, we can take it back to Jonny's room and I can shift, too. I could use some wolf time, man."

They could play. He wasn't scared of canines. In fact, he found them wickedly fun. Especially the tail-chasing part.

They got chicken and beef, and Deke got him a whole boned fish of some sort. He knew because Deke let him smell and approve each one. By the time they got back to the familiar smelling room, he was ravenous.

The air moved in waves around him, the magically-charged feel of a shift washing over him. Then Deke barked, hairy nose pushing his toward the chicken. He pounced it happily, tearing into the meat like he was starving. The wolf shared his chicken, but didn't fight him for it. Both of them were alpha enough. They didn't need to compete.

Luc ate until he was full, then his attention was captured by the swish and slide of the wolf's tail upon the floor. The tail thumped once more, twice, and then went silent. Oh. Someone wanted to play. His ears twitched, and he crouched, listening for the next motion.

The sound of licking chops came off to the right, several feet from where Deke had started out. Sneaky.

Luc turned on a dime, pounced, managing to land

squarely on the firm backside and give it a swat as he yowled. Deke barked, the sound high and surprised, before scrabbling away, the sound of something crashing to the floor loud. He chuffed happily and followed, giving chase.

He didn't need to see for this.

His feet slid in chicken grease, making him slam into furniture. That was good, though, telling him where the desk was so he could jump over it. He scrambled over the top, landing in the spinny chair.

That was odd.

He shook his head, trying to clear it.

Deke barked, the sound grounding him, giving him a place to go next. He dug into the cushion of the chair and sprang forward, reaching for the wolf with his front paws. There was only the barest hint of fur before Deke scrabbled away. When he made to follow, though, Deke took him down, crashing and tackling.

Yowling happily, he wrapped his arms around Deke's ruff, claws digging in. Deke chuffed for him, the sound weirdly lupine, and bit at his nose before struggling away.

Play.

Play.

He followed slowly, almost lazily, sated and happy.

They romped, both of them slowing down a little, both making happy noises. He had no idea how long they played before Deke started yawning. He nudged and pushed Deke until he felt the warmth of a sunbeam. There. Napping there was good. A low rumble of approval sounded, Deke curling up with him.

His purr vibrated all throughout him.

Yes.

Good.

Napping.

That was even better than chicken.

Especially when he had someone to nap with.

Jonny walked into his office and had a moment of absolute, blind panic. The blinds were open, sun streaming into the back third of the room. And the place was... ransacked. Absolutely destroyed.

He almost called for security, then he saw... two tails. Two furry tails and two furry heads and one huge cat and one wolf napping together, in the sunshine.

He slumped a little, relief making him stupid. He stepped back into the hall, hitting the button on the keypad beside the door that would summon someone to close the damned blinds. He couldn't get to the remote, which was under Deke's paw.

They had... rampaged. Eaten and played and rampaged. He couldn't wait to tell Kasey.

He might have to take pictures before he had the blinds closed. "Ah, Duke. I need a camera and then for you to get the remote for me."

Duke looked in, blinked once. "Of course, sir."

"Thank you." That was a Kodak moment, after all.

The camera was handed over, then Duke tiptoed through the wreckage, heading for the remote.

One of Deke's ears twitched, but the wolf obviously recognized his packmate, which was what Duke had quickly become. It was adorable. Thank goodness, too, because that way no one moved until after Jonny had set the camera on sports mode and taken twenty pictures in quick succession.

Luc obviously trusted Deke because, barring a half-hearted swipe to warn Duke away, his cat stayed asleep.

Once he had enough pictures to keep Kasey amused for

weeks, Jonny closed the blinds with the remote, ventured in, and nudged Luc with his toe.

Luc yowled softly the sound making him smile, and curled around his leg.

"Mmm. Hello, my cat. Did you have a good day with Deke?"

His answer was a slow, lazy stretch, fangs glinting.

"Good for you. Did you know that you destroyed my office?"

Those empty eyes blinked, then the evil little bastard chuffed, laughing. Oh, someone deserved a beating.

"I think I might have to punish you, sweet."

Deke yawned, tail thumping the floor, and Jonny glared at him. "You can see. You know better."

Deke's tongue lolled out, lazy and wet. These two were nowhere near worried enough.

"I think I'll have to call Kasey in to kick your ass," Jonny said, bending to scratch Deke's ears. "I have this one to beat."

Luc curled around his legs, teeth sharp on his heel.

"No biting."

Deke turned and nipped at his calf, and Jonny got a little toothy, growling down at them. Deke backed off, but his cat bit again.

Jonny reached down and grabbed Luc by the scruff, shaking him a bit. "Will you excuse us?" he asked Deke before dragging Luc toward the door.

Luc yowled and hissed, the sound partially shocked, partially furious. Partially curious.

"We need a bed for what I have in mind, sweet." He was going to convince Luc to shift, if he could, and then beat that muscled ass purple.

That would do them both a world of good. He could feel Luc's strength, the heat in the palm of his hand. He let Luc feel his strength, as well. His resolve. No more bored kitty. Luc growled at him, protesting, teeth snapping at the air.

Jonny shook his prize a little before tossing him into the private room, the bed fresh and clean-smelling even from the door. Perfect. Luc leapt onto the bed, pouncing right in the center of it, and roared.

"Oh, if you have something to say to me, say it as a man." He only hoped Luc could, that he could control the change.

Luc shifted, the change becoming faster each time. The man was beautiful—wild and fierce, untamed and all his. "Don't drag me."

"Then don't tear up my office." His muscles tensed, the predator in Jonny ready to pounce.

Luc snarled, fingers curling in the sheets. The cat was right there, ready to come again. Jonny circled to the other side of the bed, moving quiet as a mouse. More quietly, really. Mice could be bloody noisy.

Luc stilled, vibrating, crouching down as he listened. Yes. That was the focus, the narrow attention that Jonny needed. He let his foot slide just a bit, scraping. Luc spun around on the bed, one hand shooting out to scratch. It barely missed him, just scooping the air.

Growling, Jonny dove in, taking Luc around the waist, bowling him over. Luc needed to struggle. The long lean muscles worked, bunching and jerking, pushing against him, fighting him. It escaped Jonny's knowledge not at all, that Luc's cock was filling.

He hummed, happy to feel it, but not giving an inch. In fact, he tightened his grip and rolled them, landing on Luc's belly. Luc yowled, twisting to bite him, hard.

"No." Pulling back, Jonny flipped Luc over, smacking that hard, round ass. Luc went still for a moment, perfectly still, then Luc leaned forward and quite deliberately bit him again. Jonny bit back a laugh, knowing what Luc was asking for. He drew back and hit so hard that the shock traveled up his arm in waves.

"Jonny! Fuck!"

"Soon, love." He slapped again, knowing he required this as much as Luc, that he needed to give, needed to feel Luc respond.

He watched his cat, the long spine arcing and bending, hips swaying in rhythm with the blows. The most amazing sounds escaped from Luc, making a weird, yowling song. Jonny closed his eyes to savor it, his hearing so much more acute that way. Was that what Luc had now? The touch and smell and sound just overwhelming him?

He could feel Luc's cock, dripping and hard, wet for him, leaking on his slacks.

So lovely. Jonny opened his eyes to check the color of Luc's ass. Almost there. Rosy, but not glowing. He hit harder. Luc snarled, biting at the air, entire body stretched like a bow string.

"Yes. Love. Look at you." Well, Luc couldn't. Still, he could feel it every time Jonny's hand connected, and that was enough.

"Mate. Mate." The entire room rang with the word.

"Mine." He slapped one more time, catching the bottoms of Luc's cheeks, before flipping his cat over and grabbing the flushed cock.

"Please." The pointed chin lifted, vein beating strongly.

"Yes." Oh, fuck yes. Jonny bit down, slicing into Luc's flesh, pulling that rich, energy-filled blood into his body.

Luc's nails tore down his back in response, his shirt ripping as his cat screamed for him. Jonny grunted, his hips jerking, his whole body suffused with the pleasure of Luc's touch. Of Luc's blood. Luc's claws dug in, squeezed, pulled him closer.

Jonny stroked Luc's cock in time with the fast-beating

heart, his head swimming, his prick diamond-hard in his trousers.

"Mate. Mate!" The energy slammed through him like a runaway train, Luc's prick heavy and dripping in his hand.

Moaning, Jonny bit harder, tearing a little. Luc would heal, and they both needed so badly. Heat sprayed—on his hand, in his mouth—pouring over him.

Yes. Jonny licked the wound, letting the scent and flavor carry him into his pleasure. Luc panted underneath him, fingers moved rhythmically on his back.

"Sweet. What you do to me."

"Mmm... You're an evil beast." Luc chuffed softly.

"Am I?" He reached beneath that lithe body and felt the heat of Luc's ass.

Luc hissed, but instead of pulling again, his cat pushed into his touch. "Careful, I bite."

"I know. I like a toothy lover." Though really, he loved Luc.

"You like me." That heady purr filled the air.

"I do. More than I wish to admit." That was something of a lie.

"I wouldn't tell. It can be your secret."

"Really?" He smiled, kissing Luc's throat. "Tell me a secret to keep for you."

Luc's lips were next to his ear. "I'm scared, Mate, that I'll never see again."

Jonny nodded. "I know. I worry, too, but I believe you will heal." He did. With all of his heart.

"If I don't, you can rip my throat out."

"Hmm. Perhaps." He thought not. They would find a way to deal with this.

Luc nipped him playfully. "You would not let another do it."

"No." That was true enough. "I would not."

Luc nodded, slowly stripping his clothes away, lips and fingers on his body. "I like Deke. He plays."

"He does. He tastes good, as well." Jonny chuckled at the little growl. "Not as good as you. You're addiction.

"That's right. I'm yours." His nipple was caught between Luc's teeth and tugged.

"As I am yours, sweet. Remember that when things seem darkest."

Luc's chuckle was nearly sweet, the bite to his nipple sweeter.

"Mmm." His cat was trying to distract him, to keep him from giving pep talks, he would imagine. Smart kitty.

"Mate." His nipple was rolled in those smart teeth, so carefully.

"Yes?" He stroked Luc's hair, his fingers lingering on each little circular pattern. So lovely.

"I have you on my tongue."

"You have me however you want me, love." He could use more of that tongue, though, certainly.

"I want to taste more." His nipple was explored, the deep purrs vibrating against him. "It's different now, bigger."

"Is it? How?" He wasn't sure he understood. He wanted to, wanted to know.

"I can smell my blood in you, smell you inside my skin."

"Oh." Oh, God. That was... Jonny wanted to bite Luc again, wanted to listen to that strong heartbeat and know that Luc could smell them.

Luc's teeth dragged down over his ribs, taunting him. It was maddening. The kind of pleasure that teetered right on the edge of too much without plunging over. His cat seemed more than happy to bite and tease, to explore every square inch of skin as it was exposed.

"Luc." He put a tiny bit of warning in his voice.

He smiled as Luc shivered, that reddened ass arching.

"So beautiful." He wanted to touch even more, wanted to feel that heat. So he did, bending and reaching.

That earned him a deep, rough yowl, Luc's body rippling for him. The skin he touched was still like fire, so hot and good that Jonny stroked it again, then again. It fascinated his fingers.

"Mate." Luc's teeth tested his thigh, hard enough to bruise.

Fuck. He... oh, that felt good. So good. He let Luc do again, just to feel it shoot up his hip and spine. His nails scored Luc's ass and his cat bit again, purring loudly.

"More." He didn't even know what he was truly asking for. He just knew he needed.

"Yes, Mate." The inside of his knee was nibbled, then his wrist was taken in the hot mouth and shaken.

He moaned, his whole body burning from the inside out. Luc was going to kill him all over again. Luc pressed him down, pressed him against the mattress, tongue dragging on his skin. He bucked, trying to get closer, better. More of that rough, inhuman tongue. His cat. His. Luc purred, body heavy, solid on him as he was loved and groomed and tasted. Jonny twisted, rubbing, their skin sliding together. He was going to explode.

"Mine." He got another bite, this one deeper, sharp.

"Yes. No matter what, sweet." Jonny would keep Luc by his side and not let him damage himself.

"I want you." Luc muscled up between his thighs. "I want to be inside you when you bite again."

"Yes." He might have taken anyone else's head off for suggesting it. Not Luc. This he wanted.

"I'm inside you, in your veins." Luc leaned down, lapped at the tip of his cock, the touch almost lazy.

"You are." He jerked, his hips rolling. His cock ached.

Fucking ached.

Luc's fingers slipped over his hole, pushed in as his prick was taken into the hot mouth.

His head fell back against the pillow, his body undulating. "Luc. Sweet. Soon."

He felt Luc's purr, then that tongue slipped down, wetting his hole.

"More!" The word burst out of him, the feeling so strong it took him over.

Luc held nothing back from him, the licking and lapping lasting forever and yet only seconds before that heavy prick pushed into him, filling him up. Jonny tensed up, the unfamiliar stretch making him want to snarl and snap his fangs. Instead he held very still, letting Luc slide all the way in. Low subvocal rumbles rolled over him, sweet and obviously meant to ease. It made him smile. He relaxed into it, his hands starting to move, his hips not quite rolling.

"Mate." Luc licked up along his chest, his throat.

"Mmm. Move, lover. Move now." His fangs itched with the need to bite. Soon.

"Now. Now. I'm in you." Luc tossed his head, hips beginning to jerk, push into him in wild lunges.

"Yes." He didn't wait any longer; he just bit. Hard. The skin nearest him was Luc's upper arm, and Jonny sank his fangs in deep.

Luc's scream split the air, sharp and heated. Almost sweet. It made him buck and groan, his ass clenching around Luc's cock. He took the hot, rich blood in, Luc in him in all ways. His orgasm was secondary to the heat that flooded into him, his cat everywhere.

Jonny panted, the air cooling him, if not helping calm him. He understood why dogs did it, really. He chuckled, thinking how Luc would bite him if his cat knew Jonny was thinking dogs.

Luc purred softly, still moving slowly inside him, rocking and filling him up.

"My cat." He licked the spot he'd bitten, the tender skin bruised now, hot to the touch.

"Yours. My Mate."

"Yes. Oh, yes." They still had a lot of work ahead of them, trying to find Luc's assailants and get his sight back, but Jonny knew what really mattered. They were in each other now, bonded. All the way.

Luc would have to live with it. He would just have to.

Chapter Fifteen

The sun was down. He could smell it.

Luc followed his nose through the club, tail twitching happily. His ass burned, ached in the best way, his mate sunk into his skin.

A tiny shriek and the sound of dishes clattering to the floor told him he had startled someone. It wasn't crowded where he was, though. Just the one waitress.

Oh.

Tuna.

Yum.

He helped, licking up lost food, cleaning plates with his tongue.

"Thanks a lot, you." The girl's voice held laughter now, though, and the clink of a broom on crockery told him it was safe to walk again.

He kept wandering, sniffing as he moved, searching out Jonny's scent. He found Deke, swiping at the wolf's calves playfully.

Deke growled and laughed, before scratching his ears. "He's in the kitchen, man."

Mmm. Good scratches. He nipped at the strong fingers in thanks, then started moving again, staying low and close to the wall. The smells of the kitchen were completely disorienting, but they led him right where he could hear Jonny's voice. Someone was getting reamed.

Huh. Interesting.

He moved more carefully in here, trying to stay out of the way of the hot.

Hard fingers tangled in his ruff, Jonny's scent overwhelming the food. "Hello, my cat."

He leaned in, purring hard enough that his claws slid on the floor.

"Mmm. The chef will try for your balls if you mess up his new tile."

He chuffed. He'd dare the human to try.

"I said 'try', love.' Jonny sounded happier now, and the sound of footsteps hurrying away told him that whoever was getting a lecture was now getting away.

Jonny smelled amazing—male and warm, solid. Jonny rubbed his back, rubbed all the way down to his tail. The scritching at the base of his tail was orgasmic. He arched and rocked, his purrs vibrating all through him.

"Come, my cat. We have more business to attend." Jonny guided him with the simplest pressure of one leg against his side.

It was imminently easier to move with Jonny, and he followed without worry. His vampire would not lead him astray. Well, not this way, at any rate. Jonny moved easily, not holding back for him. Periodically he scented something in the air, was distracted for a second, then Jonny put him back on track.

Jonny finally turned toward his office, leading him with a nudge or two. Oh, that was a good sign. He might have started bouncing a bit. It was inevitable. He was a kitten, deep in his heart.

Jonny laughed at him. "I have at least three tax reports to go over, kitty. Don't get excited."

Tax reports.

He snorted.

What fun was that?

He headed for the big chair by Jonny's desk, not even

considering that it wouldn't be empty for him as he leapt. It was, and he settled in, listening to the murmur of the phone ringing, of Jonny talking to someone. His tail covered his nose and he dozed, ears twitching idly at every sound.

"Luc? Luc. Kasey thinks he has something."

His ears twitched, and he started asking questions, only realizing about halfway in that Jonny couldn't understand him.

"Come on, love. I need you here as a man." Jonny stroked his cheeks, focusing him.

He imagined himself human, male, solid. His fur melted away, his body stretching with the change.

"My beautiful cat." Jonny kissed his human mouth, smiling against it.

"Mmmm... mate." He kissed his bloodsucker back, fingers sliding up the silky material of Jonny's shirt.

"No distracting me." They pushed apart, but the way Jonny's fingers lingered on his skin told him it was reluctant.

He rumbled softly, but let Jonny go. "What did your man say?"

"He says that you do work for some very dangerous people, my love."

Luc nodded; there was no lie in that. Somehow he'd fallen into things and hadn't clawed his way out. "I tend to find trouble, or it finds me."

"Indeed. Well, Kasey thinks it is indeed the gentleman you took my files for." Jonny chuckled, a puff of air against his mouth.

"The one that hired me?" His mind was already making plans.

"Hired you. Blackmailed you. Whichever it was."

He chuffed softly. "In my line of business, those things are the same. I'll be back."

"Where are you going?" One strong hand caught him. "With no clothes?"

"I won't need clothes." He was much more effective as a cat. More pointed. And his nose worked.

"You will need eyes, love. Let us help you." Us had to mean Deke, who was suddenly just inside the door.

He bounced into the wolf, snarled softly in surprise. "I want him to pay."

"He will."

Jonny and Deke said it at the same time, Deke's hands steadying him.

The urge to just go was huge, to run out and sniff out the bastard almost painful, but... He couldn't see.

"Shh." Jonny was there, turning him back into the room, drawing him to sit. "We need a plan."

"We find him. I kill him." Was there more plan?

"Well, yes, but we cannot go rushing off."

Deke chuckled. "Jonny's trying to say we all want to end up alive but him."

He rolled his eyes. Pack mentality. It wasn't natural.

"We will find a way." Jonny sounded a little peeved.

"When?" Now worked for him.

"Soon, love."

"Chill." Deke moved farther into the room, and Luc heard the tapping of fingers on keyboard keys.

Soon. Right.

He shifted back into his true form and started pacing, tail swishing, claws digging into the carpet.

Patience was not a cat-like virtue.

Soon was not going to be soon enough.

"So, how do we get to Mic Silvia," Jonny asked, watching Luc pace.

"He moves around—there's a condo here, a suite of rooms there. Even a warehouse. He's slippery." Deke shrugged, smiled over at him. "I vote for luring him with bait."

"You're not funny." No. He was not using a blind cat for bait.

"I wasn't joking. They want Luc."

"Yes, but isn't the point here to keep him safe?" Damn it. He was not going to do it.

"That's your point," Deke pointed out. "His is to eat the guy's face. Mine is to flush the guy out."

"Toilet references." He sighed. Luc, of course, had changed back into a cat and was not helping at all.

Luc stopped still, a deep, vicious snarl sounding.

"Luc?" Jonny looked at Deke before scanning the room with all of his senses.

Deke sniffed and leapt for him even as Luc sprang for the window, claws bared.

Jonny went crashing down under Deke, struggling. Damn it, he could take care of himself.

The windows broke in, three men coming in and face to face with his cat. The sun streamed in, and it occurred to him why Deke had tackled him down behind a table. He was helpless to assist. He could hear Luc's fury, the snarls and growls sharp on his ears.

"Help him, damn it!" He knew, now. Knew he had to be just a spectator. Deke could help.

"Stay down."

Luc's claws appeared at the edge of the desk, bloody and wet. Jonny hit the alarm button. The alarm whooped into life, the lights going red. Within seconds, they would have guards there, armed to the teeth.

He heard gunshots, then screams as the unmistakable scent of blood filled the air. No. It didn't smell like Luc's blood, but he had to know. Jonny poked his head above the table, the sun burning him for those few moments. Luc and Deke were tearing at flesh, working together to bring a pair of men down. One man was running.

"Duke!" Sometimes it was hard telling who he was yelling at, with Duke and Deke together, but he saw his assistant tear by and take the man down.

Suddenly there was a cat covering him, pressing him to the ground, as fierce snarls and yowls filled the air. He quite imagined someone was telling him off.

That meant there was no real damage, he hoped. "My Luc. I do hope that is not your blood."

In answer, Luc plopped down on him and started grooming him.

Laughing, Jonny scratched those sensitive ears. "Someone fix that window, hmm?"

"We're on it." A heavy, dark blanket was draped over him and Luc.

"How did they get past my emergency shutters?" Damn it, he'd paid thousands for those things.

"I don't know yet." Deke shrugged, popped under the blanket, face scratched and streaked with blood. "Good thing Luc smelled them."

"Very good." He smiled at Deke, pulling the blanket around him more closely. "Set us up with a private room?"

"You got it." Deke growled and nodded. "Duke, man. You got this?"

"I do." Duke sounded just as growly. It was amazing, how protective they all were.

"Luc, man." Deke nudged his cat with one toe. "Let's get him somewhere safe."

Luc rumbled and slid off while Deke grabbed him up and carried him, completely covered.

Ah, this was the life. He actually chuckled, which made both of the beasts with him growl. Quite loudly.

Luc's teeth nibbled his ankles, warning him.

"What? I am traveling in style." He could feel it when they reached the windowless hallway, the sun blocked away.

"You're pushing your luck with Fuzzy back there. So, you want us to go do some interrogation? Those guys were pure muscle, but someone hired them."

He didn't have to think hard to guess who exactly that was.

"I do. I want him here, accounting for this mess." He wanted his pound of flesh and, from Luc's yowl, his cat agreed.

"Fine. We'll go do some talking and follow the trail. When we bring him in, you and Mr. Kitty can... discuss the situation."

"Thanks, Deke. Feel free to take a detail with you." He waited for Deke to leave before he turned to Luc. Luc was pacing, growling, fur all on end. "Come here, my cat."

That huge, flat head turned toward him, those empty eyes searching for him.

"Here, love." He moved closer, his fingers brushing Luc's muzzle.

Luc purred, tongue flicking out to taste him.

"That's it." That told him Luc was safe, that all he needed to do was clean his cat up. His lips twisted. Of course, getting Luc in a tub was infinitely less homicidal in human form...

"We should bathe, sweet."

Luc yowled for him, tongue sliding on his wrist.

"I know, but you are a bit... bloody." He needed to make sure Luc was all right.

He felt Luc's soft sigh and knew his cat was trying to change.

"That's it, love. Smart Deke. This room has a rather

luxurious bath." He kept talking, simply easing Luc into it. He watched every second of the transformation, fascinated by it, by the way that Luc's face changed, the way the long muscles shifted.

"Are you safe, Mate?"

"I am. I am perfectly fine." There were no windows in this room, so even if they had another breach, they were good.

Luc stood, hands reaching for his clothes. "I need to see."

The irony of Luc's words did not escape him. He helped, though, taking Luc's wrists and leading them to his shirt, letting his cat pull it off.

"They were coming to hurt you." That growl sent shivers up his spine.

"They didn't." No, his cat had protected him, blind and all.

"No." Luc nuzzled his chest, leaving a streak of blood.

"Mmm. I imagine that's not nearly as tasty as yours." He pulled Luc with him to the bath.

He used the shower head to rinse Luc, his cat muttering softly until he began filling the tub with hot, clean water. They made the water as hot as they could stand it before sinking. Yes. That would soothe all the adrenaline-sore muscles.

Luc's hands explored every inch of him, sometimes grooming, sometimes searching. He did the same, without the grooming. There were cuts and scrapes, but they were all healing well. The air was redolent with purrs, and Luc's teeth on his throat were enough to make him want to attempt that lazy, low sound himself. Jonny settled for a happy moan, a deep, rough sound. The water, his cat, the blessed heat. It was perfect.

Well, except for that nasty business about someone

believing they could invade his home. They had hopefully nipped in that the bud. Really, the club's reputation had to be upheld.

Luc bit his collarbone, teeth sharp. The feeling made his cock jump, made his nerve endings fire up. He wanted more, suddenly so hard he was shaking.

"Mine." Another bite hit him, right above his nipple.

"Scared me, love." No more scares with Luc. Maybe they should go on a holiday together.

"I protect you." Luc rubbed one cheek against his chest.

"You do." He supposed, in a way, that his sunlight weakness put him on level pegging with Luc's blindness.

"When he comes, I will kill him, too."

"We have to talk to him first, love." Really. Just in case there were more people out to get them.

Luc's eyebrows drew down, the frown fierce.

"We need to make sure he has no acquaintances who feel the same about us as he does."

"Me. This is about me." Luc sighed, fingers trailing along his arm.

"He wanted papers from my club." Luc might be collateral damage. Who knew, unless they talked to the man?

Luc nodded, a deep growl rumbling inside him. "They were willing to damage me to get it."

"They were." He wanted to tear out throats every time he thought about it. To distract himself, he stroked Luc's wet skin, fingers rubbing.

"You won't let them have me."

"You know I won't. Just as you protect me." He turned Luc's face so he could take a kiss, needing the flavor and heat.

Luc snarled, climbed up his body, rubbing all the way.

"Mmm." He gripped Luc's ass in both hands, holding them together. That way they could rock and rub and float.

"How can you be so calm?"

"What?" Jonny was far from calm. "I am not. I simply don't growl."

Luc bared his teeth. "That's unnatural."

"Kiss me." They could work out a great deal of that aggression this way.

He thought, for about a moment, that Luc would argue, then that hungry mouth crashed down on his, pressing hard enough he could taste blood in the kiss. Moaning, he pulled Luc closer, trying to get into his cat's skin. That was it. That was the way to channel the rage. He imagined he could feel the hint of claw in Luc's fingers as they scraped down his skin. The idea made him shiver, made his cock jump against Luc's skin. The water added an extra set of hands, lapping against them.

"Mate." Luc straddled him, cock hotter than the water, sliding on his belly.

"Yes." He bit at Luc's lip, a hard nip that drew more blood.

"Mine." His cock was taken in one, warm hand, rubbed against the tight hole.

"Now." Jonny knew what Luc wanted, what he needed. He pushed up, letting Luc slide down on top of him, around his cock.

He could hear those sounds—the deep, rich yowls of pleasure—for an eternity. His balls drew up, his hands clenching tight on Luc's skin, his nails digging deep. Luc's body gripped his prick, working him like a hand.

He gritted his teeth, his fangs biting into his lip. He needed to hold on, just a few moments longer. A tiny bit. He could do that.

"They can't have me. I'm staying here." Luc growled,

squeezed harder.

"I know. I am keeping you." That was all there was to it.

"Good." Claws dragged over his shoulders, his chest.

"Luc!" Jonny spent, his cock jerking madly inside the hot, tight body he loved so well.

Luc hummed, head back, feeling him. He reached down for Luc's straining prick, wanting to feel it dance for him. Wanting to feel the final push around his flesh. He let his nails drag, all the way up its length, scratching the tip just a bit. Luc grunted, heat pouring over his fingers.

"Now we're all clean, hmm?" They were, after a fashion. They were still in the water, at least.

Luc's response was a low, lazy purr.

"We need to... " The next sound from Luc was a jaw-cracking yawn, and Jonny forgot all about interrogating anyone.

Soaking was healthy, healing, and his cat needed to store his energy.

The rest would work itself out later. For now they would just luxuriate in being alive. And together.

Chapter Sixteen

Luc spent an hour grooming himself, assuring himself that every hair was in place, every claw was sharp and shiny. He wanted to be ready when he had to kill the man.

They'd gone at night, so Jonny and Kasey could kelp Deke and Duke retrieve their prey. He had wanted to go, but they had all voted him down.

He snarled softly and quietly dragged his claws along Jonny's pillow, the fluff tickling his toes.

They were going to bring the man back, though. Bring him back and question him and then give him to Luc. Jonny had promised.

They had beaten Luc.

Tortured him.

Destroyed his home.

Taken his eyes.

The man would scream.

He arched, tail flat.

He heard it, when someone came in, heard the sound of a struggle. He could smell Deke, the wolf pumped. Excited.

He headed for the door, searching carefully, it case it had moved.

After the break-in, some things had changed drastically. They took the man to Jonny's office, and he knew the way there. He could hear Luc and Deke's man, talking, and he could smell Deke, close. He did not, however, smell someone he knew.

Not Salvia, then.

"There you are, kitty-man. Hang back while they talk, huh?" He leaned over, rubbed his cheek against Deke's leg in greeting. Deke stroked his ears, the touch affectionate. "You'll get your shot. This is the contractor, so to speak. His scent was all over your place, all over the bomb. Not our guy, but... Well, you know..."

Yowling in agreement, Luc dipped his head, pushed into the touch. So long as his mate was safe.

Jonny was safe. It was the Kasey-man, Deke's mate. He was doing the talking, voice hard as steel. Luc liked that, that hardness. He wanted it to hurt.

Deke scratched his head one more time before going to answer when Kasey called him. The sound of flesh hitting flesh came soon after.

He growled, head down as he headed for the door. His mate. No hurting his mate. No, the beating sound Deke, hitting the man. That was good. He approved of every grunt and groan.

Luc found Jonny easily, leaned against his leg.

"Hello, love. He's not talking very well. I suppose we'll just have to beat him some more." Jonny sounded dispassionate, completely at ease. The advantage of having a vampire lover.

He bared his teeth in a long, slow smile, then sauntered over and nosed up along the man's leg until he found the crotch. The man screamed, which he thought was a very good start. It felt good to have the upper hand in their dealings this time. It took one good swipe to split the fabric of the man's slacks and, if he drew blood, Luc assumed it was fair. If he'd been able to see, he wouldn't miss.

Jonny chuckled, and the man started babbling, but it

wasn't in a language he understood. Wrong answer. He snarled softly, then simply tilted his head and took the soft sac in his teeth, and breathed.

"Wait! Wait! What is it you want to know? I'll tell you anything." There was fear, acrid and sour, right there in his nose. It smelled ugly.

Luc purred. Yes. Tell my mate everything.

The man began talking, Kasey guiding the questions.

He listened, idly, to the words falling down around him. Evidence. Loose ends. Withheld information. It was nonsense. In the end, it was enough to know that this was not the end of the trail.

This wasn't Salvia.

That simply wasn't good enough.

He growled softly, shaking his head from side to side, knowing it would scare, sting.

"Please! Please, I'll take you to him! I'll show you. Anything..."

Now was good for him. Incredibly good for him.

"Good." Jonny stroked his neck, calming him, pulling him gently away. "Take us."

"You leave that beast here."

Luc's hackles rose and his growl made the room shake.

"That beast is what got you into this mess in the first place." He could hear the smile in Jonny's voice. It wasn't a pleasant one. "I should let him eat your balls."

Let him? Like he took orders. He considered biting Jonny's ass, but he thought it might look bad.

Deke's chuckle told him maybe he had moved a little too close to doing just that. Maybe his mouth had even opened a tiny bit.

He snorted, tail flicking. Dogs.

Honestly.

Chapter Seventeen

Jonny loved a good hunt.

Oh, he didn't show it as much as, say, Deke. Or his bloodthirsty cat. But he loved it.

This was going to be a good hunt. He could tell.

Luc was on his leg, close, although he imagined his cat was taking cues more from Deke than him. Those two had an unholy friendship. When he had time to think about it, to discuss it with Kasey, he was sure they would both be horrified. For now, it worked.

"Okay, third floor, that lit window." Deke was relaying, Kasey across the way gathering information. "There's three of them, all armed, that he can see."

"That shouldn't be too difficult, then." Jonny stroked Luc's ears. "Promise me you will be careful, my cat."

Luc yowled softly, whiskers vibrating.

"Did I say you could not come?" No, he had never made that argument. Luc needed this.

His cat head butted him, muttering and vocalizing, and Jonny could swear he understood. How very odd. Surely he wasn't learning to speak cat...

Deke chuffed at him, laughing at him.

"Oh, stop it. Both of you." They were connected at the brain. Too bad there wasn't enough to go around.

"Yeah, yeah. So, we go upstairs, we do our business, we go home, right?"

"We do. We make sure, though, that there's no

information on Luc or me. Or you or Kasey for that matter." They would take whatever they found.

"Right. You leave that to me." Deke met his eyes. "You and Luc, you stick together."

"I'll stay with him. I promise." He heard the little growl, but he couldn't lie. Luc would need his eyes.

He touched Luc's neck and they headed in, Luc's form a bare shadow on the stairs.

Jonny opened his senses, listening for the telltale heartbeats of the guards. If he could pinpoint them now, it would be a great help. There was one on the stairs Kasey hadn't seen, and he moved with Luc to take the man out, blood splashing soundlessly.

Jonny loved to watch Luc hunt. Even without his eyes, Luc was a fine stalker, and his claws and teeth were sharp as razors. He had no doubt that his cat could defend them, the club, him, with little trouble at all.

That time would come. For now, they needed to remove the biggest threat to their safety. Then they could work on healing Luc, on getting to know each other's quirks. Jonny couldn't wait. They slipped upstairs together, moving faster now. The door was there, Deke growling softly, warning them.

Jonny pushed Luc to one side of the door, letting Deke take the other. He nodded to Deke through the gloom, ready for the big wolf to break down the door.

He heard Kasey through Deke's earphones. "They know you're there."

Luc didn't wait. The big cat snarled and hit the door, full force, slamming back into whoever was unfortunate enough to be in front. Jonny didn't have time to spare for thinking about whether it was a trap. He simply stormed in, taking one guard by the shoulder and ripping his throat out.

He could hear screams, shots, then the snarls and

growls from his cat. Deke roared, the sound of flesh hitting flesh closer than he would have expected. Jonny fought to get to Luc, needing to know his lover was well.

Luc had someone that he remembered, only vaguely, pinned full-body against the window, teeth snapping about the man's scarred, round face. The man had been at the club once, maybe twice as a guest of someone. He'd wanted to become a member. Jonny had turned him down. Simple. Easy. Painless. The whole scene flashed through his head that quickly.

But it wasn't fucking Salvia.

Not Salvia.

Why had this man attacked Luc? The club? Did Salvia hire him? Why all these layers? Why all the blasted drama? Why...

He strode forward to ask one or all of those questions, when the glass all around the man cracked, the panes shattering as if in slow motion before disappearing and falling through. They all stood for what seemed to be an eternity, time stopping completely before it started up again, the heavy weight of the man seemingly sucked out through the empty pane, hanging in the thick night air before gravity took hold. It was only then that he could move. The thin, high scream as the man plummeted toward the ground gave him the impetus to leap forward and grab Luc, his hands clutching at fur and muscle. No losing his cat. No. Luc arched back, weight twisting to help him, to keep them in.

For a moment - and, later, he quite thought that it was the longest moment of his life - he thought that his hands would not have the strength, that his beloved cat would follow out into the altogether-too-close-to-full-moonlit night.

His fingers held, however, and Luc's claws dug into the carpeting, refusing to release until Deke hauled them back in the window, so that all of them could collapse on the floor. Their prey, unfortunately, was a complete loss.

"You lot all right?" Kasey asked, voice crackling in his earphone. "I have to tell you, there's a very... mushy man leaking onto a Subaru out here. It's a touch awkward."

Ass.

"Deke? Is everyone... functional?"

They all panted in unison, then Luc yowled an affirmative, the sound sharp and aggravated.

"I'm sorry, love. I know you had plans for him." So had Jonny. Damn it all, he'd wanted his information. He hated being in the dark. Well, metaphorically.

Luc huffed and snorted, muzzle moving over his jaw and neck, making sure he was solid.

"I am well, my cat. Are you cut?"

Luc's answer was a very clear 'no'.

"Good." Good. Deke was fine. A quick glance told him that people were gathering below, however.

"Kasey. What is our easiest route out?"

"Down. There's a connecting tunnel to this building. I'll meet you there."

"Down it is." They could easily take the stairs, even with Luc's blindness. His cat was sure-footed.

They moved together, after Deke and Jonny swept the room for information, heading into the inky blackness. Deke carried a sheaf of papers and folders, but Jonny had a distinct suspicion that they were the ones Luc had taken from his office the night they'd made their bargain. What an unexpected pleasure that had turned out to be.

His mind questioned how this unknown had come into possession of the information, but only for the briefest moment as Jonny let his eyes drag down the long, sleek line of his cat, his mate, his Luc. As if Luc felt it, that heavy tail twitched. He had time to discover those irritating details.

He had, in fact, an eternity.

"I can smell you, Jonny. Please let us get down the stairs and out of here before you guys start humping."

Really, Deke could be so rude. Luc agreed, apparently, one heavy paw swooping out to snag Deke's ankle. Deke cackled, and Jonny could see the flash of his teeth in the dark. When they burst out of the stairwell, the low light was almost blinding.

Kasey was there, pulling them into another tunnel, moving them faster. Jonny made sure Luc was keeping up, but it didn't seem to be a problem. There were no obstacles, no bits of debris to trip him up. His cat was quite stunning, more than capable of hunting—eyes or no. The thought reassured him. Luc seemed to understand this instinctively, and Jonny's worries that Luc would harm himself eased.

If nothing else, his mate would stay until Salvia was… dealt with.

"Keep walking. What happened up there?" Kasey sounded agitated.

"A window broke."

"It broke." Kasey blinked back at him.

"Yeah, baby." Deke backed him up. "Luc didn't even throw the guy at it hard."

Luc's muzzle split in a happy smile that simply dripped with maliciousness. Not hard at all. Jonny shook his head.

"Fascinating." Kasey did have a fine grasp of sarcasm.

"Well, you know how it goes." Jonny patted Kasey's ass, eliciting another growl from his Luc, which led to Kasey snapping idly at his mate, who hissed.

Deke chuffed. "Don't worry, Luc. Kasey's not into eating pussy."

Oh, that was terrible. Jonny laughed, trying to keep

the noise down. He felt oddly light, happy, in spite of what had happened, what was sure to happen. Kasey started chuckling, then Deke, and it was all over. They had to stop, all of them shaking with mirth.

That was when Jonny decided it didn't matter who was after them or what would happen in the future. He had the best friends a man could ask for. They could get through anything together.

And if they didn't, his mate would simply shove any offenders out a window.

Codes and Roses

Breinigsville, PA USA
27 July 2010
242474BV00006B/2/P